Jessica's not kidding around . . .

"Come back inside!" *Jessica heard Mr. Clark's voice bellow over the noise of the bulldozer.* "Come back inside right now!"

Jessica looked behind her again and saw Mr. Clark, Mrs. Knight, Mr. Sweeney, and several other teachers chasing the students.

More and more kids were pouring out of the school now. The pro-soccer faction was chasing the teachers. Lila, Janet, Peter, Aaron, Bruce, Denny, and dozens of other kids were streaming out of the doors.

Jessica raced past the bulldozer and saw the driver do a double take when he saw her and all the other kids running behind her.

She ran over to a tree, reached into her backpack, and removed a bicycle chain and padlock.

SNAP! went the lock as Jessica chained herself to the trunk of the tree, wrapping the chain around her waist and the thick trunk. "Now try to bulldoze this tree!" *she yelled at the driver.*

Sweet Valley Twins titles, published by Bantam Books.
Ask your bookseller for titles you have missed:

SWEET VALLEY TWINS

Jessica Saves The Trees

◇

Written by
Jamie Suzanne

Created by
FRANCINE PASCAL

BANTAM BOOKS
TORONTO • NEW YORK • LONDON • SYDNEY • AUCKLAND

JESSICA SAVES THE TREES
A BANTAM BOOK 0 553 40690 6

Originally published in U.S.A. by Bantam Skylark Books

First publication in Great Britain

PRINTING HISTORY
Bantam edition published 1993

Sweet Valley High and Sweet Valley Twins are registered
trademarks of Francine Pascal.

Conceived by Francine Pascal.

Produced by Daniel Weiss Associates, Inc.,
33 West 17th Street, New York, NY 10011

Bantam Books are published by Transworld Publishers Ltd.,
61–63 Uxbridge Road, Ealing, London W5 5SA,
in Australia by Transworld Publishers (Australia) Pty. Ltd.,
15–25 Helles Avenue, Moorebank, NSW 2170,
and in New Zealand by Transworld Publishers (N.Z.) Ltd.,
3 William Pickering Drive, Albany, Auckland.

Printed and bound in Great Britain by
Cox & Wyman Ltd., Reading, Berks.

One

◇

"If I hear one more word about your being a famous television celebrity, I'm going to throw up," Lila Fowler said to Jessica Wakefield as the two sixth-graders hurried toward the bleachers of the Sweet Valley Middle School soccer field.

"You're just jealous," Jessica replied.

"Ha!" Lila practically shouted, coming to a dead stop in the middle of the crowded school lawn. "I'm just sick of listening to you brag all the time."

A few weeks earlier, Jessica's twin sister, Elizabeth, had accidentally gotten locked in the stairwell of an empty hotel. Jessica had led the police and her parents to the rescue, and the story had been featured on the evening news. It had turned Jessica into a local hero for a short time afterward.

"I said it before and I'll say it again," Jessica

said with a satisfied smile. "You're jealous."

Lila stamped her foot on the ground. "Stop saying that."

"Why are you two just standing there?" Grace Oliver asked as she and Tamara Chase hurried past them toward the bleachers. "The soccer scrimmage is going to start in a few minutes."

"Did you hear that the guys are going to be dedicating their goals to their favorite girls?" Tamara added excitedly. "Janet Howell told us."

"Awesome!" Jessica said happily. "We're coming." She tugged on Lila's sleeve. "Come on, let's get seats. They're not going to wait for us to get there to start—even if I am *a famous television celebrity*," she added. Sometimes it was so much fun to irritate Lila.

All around them, kids were streaming from the school building to the soccer field, rushing to get good seats on the bleachers.

But Lila didn't move. "I'm not taking one step until we get something straight, Jessica Wakefield. I am *not* jealous of you. I'm not jealous of anybody. If anything, you're jealous of *me*."

"Jealous of you? What are you talking about?" Jessica demanded. "*I'm* the only Unicorn who's ever been on television."

The Unicorns were a club made up of all the prettiest and most popular girls at Sweet Valley Middle School. Jessica and Lila were both members.

Even though Lila was Jessica's best friend, she

was also her biggest rival. And the truth was, Jessica had lots of reasons to be jealous of Lila. Lila was the daughter of one of the wealthiest people in Sweet Valley, and as far as Jessica was concerned, Lila's father spoiled her rotten. Lila had more clothes, more vacations, more spending money, more everything than any other girl at school. Ever since Jessica could remember, Lila had been showing her up.

But Lila had never been on television, and Jessica was going to make the most of it.

Just then Elizabeth came hurrying past Jessica.

"Hey!" Jessica said, grabbing Elizabeth by the arm. "You're going in the wrong direction. The game is on the soccer field. Why are you running toward school?"

Elizabeth was wearing jeans, a sweatshirt, and a baseball cap with a button that said "PRESS" on it. The face underneath the cap was identical to Jessica's. Both girls had the same long, sun-streaked blond hair, the same blue-green eyes, the same tiny dimple in their left cheeks. But that was just the outside.

On the inside, the identical Wakefield twins were as different as night and day. Jessica loved excitement and attention and being a member of the Unicorns. She loved excitement so much that she frequently managed to get herself into a lot of trouble. And she always depended on her sister to help get her out of it.

Elizabeth was hardworking and responsible. Unlike Jessica, she actually enjoyed schoolwork. She spent a lot of time reading, and she also wrote for *The Sixers*, the official sixth-grade newspaper she had started.

"Todd Wilkins just told me that Mr. Bowman wants to see me in his office," Elizabeth explained. "It's something about *The Sixers*. Mr. Bowman told him it was important."

Mr. Bowman was the sixth-grade English teacher and the faculty adviser to *The Sixers*.

"Maybe he wants you to start reporting more about the Unicorns," Jessica said with a laugh.

Elizabeth laughed too. The Unicorns were always trying to get Elizabeth to write about them in the paper. But according to Elizabeth, shopping and gossiping weren't exactly newsworthy activities.

Elizabeth looked down at her watch. "I'd better hurry if I'm going to make it back for the game."

Lila rolled her eyes. "You sure do take your newspaper seriously."

"I have to," Elizabeth said. "I'm the editor-in-chief. If I don't take it seriously, I can't expect the readers to, either." She adjusted her backpack and started off toward the school. "I'll see you guys at the scrimmage."

Jessica plucked again at Lila's sleeve. "Come on, or we might not get a seat," she said. "You wouldn't want a famous television celebrity to be seen standing up, would you?" she joked.

"Arrrgh," Lila muttered. "I'm *so* sick of hearing about you being on television."

"That's because you're *jealous*," Jessica said with a satisfied smile.

"Come in," Mr. Bowman said in his deep voice, opening his office door.

A lady that Elizabeth had never seen before was sitting in the chair beside Mr. Bowman's desk.

Elizabeth shot a puzzled look at Mr. Bowman. "You wanted to see me?"

Mr. Bowman nodded. "Yes. I wanted you to meet Mrs. Simmons. Mrs. Simmons owns the Sweets for the Sweet shop on Elm Street."

Elizabeth felt her cheeks grow a little warm. Two weeks before, she had written a scathing article on the Sweets for the Sweet shop. Dennis Cookman and Alex Betner, two boys from Sweet Valley Middle School, had gone there one afternoon, and the owner had refused to let them come into the shop. According to Dennis, the owner had said it was because she didn't like kids. Elizabeth noticed that Mrs. Simmons was holding a copy of *The Sixers*. "Did you write this story?" Mrs. Simmons demanded angrily, waving the newspaper.

"Yes, I did," Elizabeth replied softly.

"Well, it's a bunch of lies," Mrs. Simmons snapped.

"A few weeks ago, didn't you tell two boys they couldn't come in your shop?" Elizabeth asked.

"Yes," Mrs. Simmons said. "I refused to let them come in because the last time they came into my store, they started a food fight!"

"A food fight!" Elizabeth exclaimed.

"Yes," the lady said. "They made such a mess I had to close my shop to clean it up. I lost a lot of business that afternoon. And now I'll lose more business, because kids will read this paper and won't want to come to my shop."

"I didn't know about the food fight," Elizabeth said in a stricken voice. "Dennis just told me you said you didn't like kids."

"I said I don't like kids *who throw food around my shop*," Mrs. Simmons retorted. "Who would?"

Mr. Bowman knitted his brows. "Did you interview Mrs. Simmons to get her side of the story before you wrote your article, Elizabeth?"

Elizabeth shook her head. "No. I guess I should have . . . but . . . I just got so mad when Dennis and Alex told me what had happened, and it seemed so unfair, that I . . . I . . ." Elizabeth trailed off weakly.

"You didn't check your facts," Mr. Bowman finished for her.

"Newspapers are supposed to present both sides of the story fairly," Mrs. Simmons said. "Even school newspapers."

"Mrs. Simmons is right," Mr. Bowman said.

"I'll print a correction as soon as possible," Elizabeth promised. "And I'm really, really sorry."

Mr. Bowman smiled. "The news business is

tricky, Elizabeth. I know you meant well, but you always have to get the facts. You can't jump to conclusions. And try to keep your personal feelings out of it. It's easier said than done, but reporters have to be objective."

"Those boys took advantage of you," Mrs. Simmons said, still angry. "And they took advantage of me."

Mr. Bowman nodded. "Lots of people try to manipulate the press, Elizabeth. You have to be on your guard about that."

"I wish there was something I could do to make it up to Mrs. Simmons," Elizabeth said unhappily.

Mr. Bowman rubbed his chin. "Perhaps the school can do something. We have several teachers' meetings during the year, and we always try to provide refreshments. Next time we have a meeting, I'll ask our school principal to order from you. Would that prove that we're serious about our apology?"

Mrs. Simmons smiled and stood. "That would be very nice."

Mr. Bowman stood up too and looked at his watch. "Wow! It's later than I thought. Elizabeth, you'd better hurry out to the soccer field. The scrimmage is about to start. I assume *The Sixers* is going to be covering it."

"Yes, sir," Elizabeth said, standing up quickly.

Mr. Bowman smiled at Mrs. Simmons. "We're very proud of our boys' soccer team," he said.

"They were undefeated last year, and that means that this year they'll be competing in Division A."

"Division A?" Mrs. Simmons repeated.

"The statewide competition," Mr. Bowman explained. "Today's scrimmage is a tryout for places on the team."

"That's nice," Mrs. Simmons said.

"That's *great*!" Mr. Bowman corrected. Then he looked a little embarrassed at getting so carried away. He gave a little cough. "You'll have to excuse me. I'm a big soccer fan."

Elizabeth couldn't help giggling as she hurried out the door. *Objective, huh?* "Don't worry, Mr. Bowman," she said. "The whole school has soccer fever. It was nice to meet you, Mrs. Simmons. And I'm really sorry about my mistake."

"Remember, Elizabeth, a reporter's job is to report," Mr. Bowman reminded her.

"Yes, sir," Elizabeth said. "I'll try to remember that." She began to jog toward the side door, then she saw a familiar figure coming out of the girls' bathroom. "Amy!" Elizabeth called out.

Amy Sutton was Elizabeth's best friend and also a member of *The Sixers* staff. "Hi," Amy said. "Ready to go to the scrimmage?"

Elizabeth nodded. "Do me a favor, will you? Take your notebook and help me keep track of the stats on the players. I'm finding out that it's hard to take notes, stay objective, and keep your facts straight all at the same time."

"What are you talking about?" Amy asked.

"I'm not sure I trust myself anymore."

"*Goooo!*" Jessica screamed at the top of her lungs.

Aaron Dallas raced down the field, and Jessica held her breath and crossed her fingers for luck. Aaron ran toward the soccer ball, caught it with his toe, and kicked it across the goal line.

"Hooray!" Jessica shouted.

All around her, kids were cheering and whistling. Immediately Aaron turned toward the bleachers and waved at Jessica. Then he gave her the thumbs-up sign.

Jessica's heart lifted. Aaron Dallas was the only sixth-grade boy to score a goal so far, and he was *her* boyfriend. Or sort-of boyfriend, anyway.

"How romantic," Tamara said with a sigh, gazing at Jessica with admiring eyes.

Jessica could feel people all around her watching her, and she flushed with pleasure.

Suddenly there was a roar from the crowd, and Jessica turned her attention back to the field just in time to see Aaron steal the ball and dribble up the field for another goal.

"Hooray!" Jessica shouted again, jumping to her feet along with the rest of the crowd. Then her heart leapt as Aaron turned toward the bleachers. His eyes swept the stands, and when they rested on Jessica, he gave her the thumbs-up sign again.

Jessica was thrilled beyond description. Not only was she the only sixth-grade girl to have a goal dedicated to her, she was the only girl in any grade to have *two* goals dedicated to her.

She heard a sigh from her right. When she turned, she was amazed to see the entire row of Unicorns staring at her in awe. *They're all jealous*, Jessica thought happily.

Jessica decided to make the most of her opportunity. She put a big smile on her face and made a show out of waving back to Aaron.

"Be careful your arm doesn't fall off," Lila said in an acid tone of voice.

Jessica lowered her arm and sat back down in her seat. She wasn't the least bit bothered by Lila's tone. It just meant Lila was jealous.

There was another shout from the crowd, and Jessica saw Denny Jacobson, an eighth-grader, score a goal.

Next to her, she noticed Janet sit up straighter. Janet had had a crush on Denny Jacobson for a long time. Jessica knew that Janet was expecting Denny to dedicate his goal to her. But instead he turned and dedicated the goal to Mrs. Montgomery, an eighth-grade English teacher.

There was a burst of laughter from the row behind the Unicorns.

"I don't get it," Jessica heard Ellen Riteman whisper. "Why did Denny dedicate his goal to Mrs. Montgomery?"

"Because Denny flunked his English test last week," Kimberly Haver whispered back.

"So far, it looks as if I'm the only Unicorn who's had a goal dedicated to her," Jessica commented, unable to resist the temptation to rub it in.

"Too bad it was dedicated by a sixth-grader," Janet retorted.

"Why is that?" Jessica asked hotly.

"Because sixth-graders never make the team," Janet answered with an insincere smile. "Last year, the team was all seventh- and eighth-graders. The sixth-graders always try out, but they never make the team."

"That's right," Lila piped up. "By tomorrow everyone will have forgotten all about Aaron's goals."

Not if I can help it, Jessica decided with a frown.

Two

◇

"Get a life, Jessica," Elizabeth said. "I'm not going to print that. It's not news." It was after dinner the next evening, and Amy and Elizabeth were sitting in Elizabeth's room, with the notes for the next day's edition of *The Sixers* spread out in front of them.

"*Not news!*" Jessica cried indignantly. "*Not news* that Aaron Dallas, who is sort of unofficially my official boyfriend, scored three goals and dedicated them to me, *and* was the only sixth-grader in recent memory to make the team? *Not news* that I, Jessica Wakefield, was the only Unicorn to have any goals dedicated to her? *Not news* that all the other Unicorns, especially Lila, were green with envy?"

"*The Sixers* is a serious newspaper, not a gossip column," Elizabeth said.

"That's not gossip," Jessica argued. "Those are facts. Why are you being so nasty about it?"

"Because Mr. Bowman told Elizabeth to be more careful about reporting news objectively," Amy answered.

"No way," Jessica said in surprise.

Amy and Elizabeth quickly filled Jessica in on what Dennis and Alex had done.

"That's awful," Jessica said when she heard the whole story. "I guess you'd better set the record straight."

"I know," Elizabeth said unhappily. "I'm working on my corrected story right now. Amy, what did you think of it?"

"It's pretty good. But I've added a few paragraphs," Amy said. She handed Elizabeth back her story.

Elizabeth ran her eyes down the page, then looked up at Amy. "But you've called Dennis and Alex 'a pair of low-down, lying, slimy, food-fighting finks.'"

"That's great!" Jessica said, clapping her hands.

"No, it's not," Elizabeth said with a frown. "That's not being objective. That's being emotional. We have to write the facts and let people decide for themselves that Dennis and Alex are a pair of low-down, lying, slimy, food-fighting finks."

"I guess you're right." Amy sighed. "You work on that, and I'll work on the story about today's scrimmage."

"You mean the story about Aaron dedicating three goals to me?" Jessica asked hopefully.

Elizabeth laughed. "The story is that Aaron Dallas made three goals and was the only sixth-grader to make the boys' team—not that he dedicated the goals to you."

"I don't see why you're always leaving me out of your stories," Jessica complained. "I'm the biggest celebrity at Sweet Valley Middle School. People are interested in reading about me. And besides," she added with a mischievous grin, "if you wrote a story about me, Lila would be *so* jealous."

Elizabeth laughed again. "So that's it. Forget about it, Jessica. I'm not going to let you use my newspaper just to compete with Lila."

Jessica flopped facedown on Elizabeth's bed and groaned. "What's the use of having a sister who's the editor-in-chief of the sixth-grade newspaper if you won't put me in it?"

"I'm the editor of the *news*paper," Elizabeth pointed out. "That means I'm in charge of printing news. If *you* had made three goals, I would mention it in the paper. I'll put you in the news when you do something newsworthy."

"Did I ever tell you about the time I was on television . . ." Jessica began.

"Get a life!" Amy and Elizabeth shouted together.

"OK, I've got it," Jessica said, coming into

Elizabeth's bedroom half an hour later. She looked down at her notebook and cleared her throat. "Here's my idea for a headline. 'Sixth-Grader Makes Team by Scoring Three Goals for Jessica Wakefield!'"

Elizabeth and Amy both groaned.

"No!" Elizabeth barked. "Come on, Jess. Don't you ever give up?"

"'Jessica Wakefield Predicts Great Division-A Season,'" Jessica tried.

"Forget it," Elizabeth said.

"How about this? 'Jessica Wakefield and Aaron Dallas Make Great Team Off the Field.'"

"Here's another idea," Amy countered. "'Newspaper Editor Kills Obnoxious Publicity-Hungry Sister.'"

Later that evening Jessica twirled happily into the living room. "I just got off the phone with Lila. And she said tons of nasty things."

Steven looked up curiously from watching television. A large bowl of popcorn sat on the floor beside him. "You seem happy about it," he commented.

"I am."

Steven shook his head in confusion. "Why would you be happy that Lila is saying nasty things?"

"Because it means she's so jealous, she's about to pop."

"What's she so jealous about?" Steven asked.

Jessica sat down beside him and reached for a

handful of popcorn. "Because Aaron Dallas made the boys' soccer team," Jessica answered.

"She's jealous of Aaron?"

"No, silly. She's jealous of me—because Aaron is sort of my boyfriend and he dedicated three goals to me this afternoon."

Steven rolled his eyes. "Unicorns," he said with a disgusted snort.

But Jessica wasn't listening. "Shhh," she said quickly as a close-up of Lois Lattimer appeared on the screen with Bob Baskins, the totally cool host of *Teen Talk*.

"I love Lois Lattimer," Jessica said as she grabbed the remote control from Steven and turned up the sound. "She's my favorite actress."

"So, Lois," Bob Baskins said. "What have you been doing since you finished shooting your last movie?"

Lois Lattimer smiled into the camera. "Well, I took part in a big environmental rally in Northern California. I did some volunteer work for the museum. And I organized the local political campaign for the congressman from my district."

"Wow, Lois, you're really active in a lot of good causes," Bob Baskins said with admiration.

"That's what I'm here today to talk about, Bob—getting active."

"Getting active, as in activism?"

Lois nodded. "I just wanted to remind kids that there's more to life than popularity and clothes and money. I want to encourage them to get involved.

Kids, you'll be amazed at what you can accomplish when you stop thinking 'me' and start thinking 'we.' When communities work together, exciting things happen. And there's nothing more exciting than improving your school, your town, your community, and your planet."

Lois Lattimer smiled into the camera and shook her long blond hair off her shoulders. Her blue-green eyes were almost the exact same shade as Jessica's, and Jessica noted happily that she was wearing a purple T-shirt with a tree on it. SAVE THE TREES was emblazoned across the T-shirt.

"Remember, kids, you're the future of California. Don't wait for grown-ups to set an example for you. Set an example for them. When grown-ups see kids caring about something and working hard to accomplish it, they'll start to care about it too."

"So your message is that activism is in," Bob Baskins said.

"That's my message," Lois replied with a smile.

The camera pulled back, and Jessica sucked in her breath when she saw that Rick Reynolds was seated right next to Lois on the sofa. Rick Reynolds was a handsome ice-hockey player and Lois Lattimer's boyfriend. Jessica had read about their romance in all the movie magazines.

The camera moved in for a close-up. Rick smiled, and Jessica felt her heart flutter. She had a huge crush on Rick Reynolds. All the Unicorns did.

"Everybody needs to get active," Rick Reynolds said.

The camera pulled back to encompass all three of them, and Jessica watched Rick put his arm over Lois's shoulder. "Lois is a beautiful woman. But it's not just her face that makes me love her. Caring about important causes is what makes a woman beautiful."

"Caring about important causes makes everybody beautiful," Lois said, smiling into the camera. "So come on, kids. Sign up. Volunteer. Or start a movement of your own. Apathy is out. Activism is in. And take it from me: activism is fun."

Jessica sighed happily. Lois was right. Activism was in. All the really cool actors and rock stars had some kind of cause they supported. A famous television celebrity like herself should have a cause too.

Later that night Jessica was on her way to the kitchen for a glass of milk before bed when one of the framed photographs on the wall of the living room caught her eye.

It was a picture of her parents taken a long time ago. They were standing with a large group of people, and everybody around them looked happy and excited.

"I thought I heard somebody out here," Jessica heard her father say.

Mr. and Mrs. Wakefield came out of the kitchen,

wearing their bathrobes. Mr. Wakefield had a glass of juice in his hand, and Mrs. Wakefield was nibbling on a cookie.

"What are you looking at?" Mrs. Wakefield asked.

"This old picture of you guys," Jessica answered.

Her parents came closer and peered over Jessica's shoulder at the photograph on the wall.

"See how young we look," Mrs. Wakefield said with a smile.

"We *were* young," Mr. Wakefield said, smiling back. "We were in college. I hadn't even thought about law school when that was taken."

"Gosh, it seems like a long time ago," Mrs. Wakefield said.

"What's going on in this picture?" Jessica asked. "Who are all those people? And why does everybody look like they're cheering?"

"They *are* cheering," Mr. Wakefield said. "That picture was taken at a student rally for better government."

"No, I think it was taken at the rally for improved education," Mrs. Wakefield corrected him.

Mr. Wakefield snapped his fingers. "No. That picture was taken at the demonstration on behalf of the striking cafeteria workers."

"Are you sure?" Mrs. Wakefield asked.

"Wow," Jessica said. "You guys were really into a lot of rallies and demonstrations. I guess activism was in when you guys were young too."

Mr. Wakefield laughed and ruffled Jessica's hair. "Activism for good causes is always in."

"And if it's not," Mrs. Wakefield added, "it should be."

"Don't stay up too late," Mr. Wakefield said as he began to climb the stairs.

"I won't," Jessica promised.

She turned back to the photograph. Her mom sure had looked pretty. And her dad looked really handsome too. Maybe caring about causes really did make people beautiful.

Three

"Hi, Jessica," Aaron Dallas said the next morning, smiling shyly at her.

"Hi." Jessica felt her cheeks turn pink. Now that Aaron was officially on the team, he seemed more grown up, and it made her feel a little shy around him. After all, he was a Division-A player now, and that made him practically a soccer hero.

Two eighth-grade girls walked by with players from the soccer team. They were holding on to the guys' arms, and it looked incredibly cool in a retro, nineteen-fifties kind of way.

"Ready to go to your first-period class?" Aaron asked.

All around them, kids were streaming through the halls, heading toward their classrooms.

"Sure," Jessica responded.

Aaron held out his arm, and Jessica looked at him, confused for a moment. Then she realized he was offering it to her to hold on to while they walked down the hall.

Jessica proudly took his arm. She couldn't help darting glances to the right and left as they walked down the hall, to see who was watching.

To her right she saw Lila and Janet, whispering and darting jealous looks in her direction.

Janet Howell was not only an eighth-grader—she was also the president of the Unicorns. That meant she was practically the most important girl at Sweet Valley Middle School, and sometimes she could be very bossy and mean. And since Janet was Lila Fowler's cousin, whenever Lila and Jessica got into a competition, Janet usually took Lila's side.

Jessica was glad that they were both there to see her walking down the hall holding on to Aaron's arm. Jessica waved, to make sure they saw her. "Hi, Lila! Hi, Janet!" she chirped.

Lila's face darkened, and Janet's lips tightened angrily. In fact, they looked jealous enough to scream, Jessica thought happily.

"So what did you think about having three goals dedicated to you?" Aaron asked her.

Jessica grinned. "I thought it was great. I thought you were great too."

Aaron grinned back. "Thanks. I'm going to dedicate more goals to you this season," he promised.

Jessica sucked in her breath. It was like a dream

come true. She closed her eyes and imagined a whole season of goals dedicated to her. Lila would die, simply die.

Aaron stopped at the door of Jessica's classroom. "See you at assembly, third period."

"Bye," Jessica said, giving him her brightest smile. She threw a glance back over her shoulder at Lila to make sure she was still watching.

"Hey, Elizabeth!" Dennis Cookman said angrily, running to catch up with her as she hurried toward the auditorium. "Why did you trash me and Alex in *The Sixers*?" he demanded.

"I didn't trash you," Elizabeth protested. "I was completely objective."

"You think calling us a pair of 'low-down, lying, slimy, food-fighting finks' is *objective*?" Dennis practically shouted.

"*Oh, no!*" Elizabeth gasped, snatching that morning's edition of *The Sixers* from his grasp. "Oh, no! How did this version get in here?"

"Elizabeth," a deep voice said in an ominous tone.

Elizabeth looked up and saw Mr. Bowman glaring down at her. "Please see me in my office after the assembly," he said.

"Yes, sir," Elizabeth answered softly.

"May I have your attention, please?" Mr. Clark said in a deep voice as he stepped onto the stage of the school auditorium.

"Gosh," Aaron said. "Mr. Clark sure does look serious."

"Mr. Clark always looks serious," Jessica answered. But Aaron was right. Mr. Clark looked even more serious than usual, and kind of unhappy, too.

"First of all," Mr. Clark said, "I'd like to commend all the players who worked so hard at the scrimmage, and congratulate all the boys who made the team."

There was a loud burst of enthusiastic applause from the audience. Jessica joined in. Behind her, somebody let out a loud, shrill whistle.

Mr. Clark held up his hands. "Settle down. Quiet, please."

When the auditorium was silent again, he took a breath, and his face furrowed in a deep frown. "Unfortunately we have received a little bad news. An official from the California Soccer Association contacted me late yesterday afternoon. Our soccer field, as it turns out, is three yards short of regulation size. The girls' season can proceed as planned. They were not scheduled to compete in Division A this year, and therefore they are not required to play on a Division-A-standard field. But I'm afraid that the boys' Division A games that we have scheduled for this season cannot be played on our field."

An unhappy groan rose from the audience.

"I know how you feel," Mr. Clark said quickly. "It's disappointing."

A hand shot up in the row in front of Jessica.

"Randy?" Mr. Clark said, nodding his head in the direction of Randy Mason, the president of the sixth-grade class.

"Can't we borrow the field at Sweet Valley High?"

"I'm afraid not," Mr. Clark said. "Their field is booked solid."

"What about the field at the park?" Janet asked from her seat a few rows over.

"I've been on the phone since yesterday afternoon, trying to locate an available field," Mr. Clark answered. "But every field in the area is booked solid for the entire season."

"You mean we're not going to get to have a season?" Peter Jefferies asked in an incredulous voice. Peter was an eighth-grader and the captain of the boys' soccer team. He was sitting with several of the other boys from the team.

Suddenly the whole auditorium was filled with shouts and protests.

"This is terrible!" Peter yelled. "If we can't have a season, that means we don't really have a team."

"It's not fair," someone shouted angrily. "They finally made Division A. They have to have a season. You have to do something."

Jessica was just as horrified as the other students. Could she possibly lose a whole season of goals dedicated to her, and the resulting popularity, because of the dumb field?

"Settle down. Settle down," Mr. Clark warned.

Reluctantly the students became quiet again.

"I asked an engineer to come survey our field this morning and see what can be done about enlarging it to regulation size. The cost would be five thousand dollars. I immediately contacted the school board. I'm sorry, but they have categorically refused to spend the money. There simply is no room for a project like that in this year's budget."

"But, Mr. Clark," Denny Jacobson protested, "you mean you're just going to give up on the season? Give up on the team? Tell us to wait until next year? Eighth-graders won't have a next year. For us, there's only this year."

Mr. Clark removed his glasses and rubbed his eyes. Jessica thought she had never seen him look so disappointed. "I know. And I'm truly sorry. The boys have worked hard to get this far. It's a shame to get so close and then have it fall apart like this."

Randy stood up. "What if we raised the money ourselves?" he asked.

Mr. Clark frowned. "Five thousand dollars is a lot of money. And you'd have only one week."

"But what if we *could* do it? Could we enlarge the field then?"

"Well, of course," Mr. Clark answered.

"Then let's see if we can all raise the money," Randy said.

"How do you propose to do it?" Mr. Clark asked.

"We'll ask for donations," Randy answered. "We'll go door to door, and ask people at the mall."

Mr. Clark shook his head. "I don't mean to discourage you, but I just don't think it can be done."

"How do we know unless we try?" Randy pointed out. "We'll make it our school cause."

Suddenly Lois Lattimer's words rang in Jessica's head.

"Who wants to volunteer to help?" Randy asked.

Jessica raised her hand so fast, she practically shot up out of her seat. All around her, hands were waving in the air. The whole auditorium began to clap and whistle.

Lois Lattimer was right, Jessica thought happily. Activism was definitely in. And Sweet Valley Middle School was ready to get active.

"Calling people names is not being objective," Mr. Bowman said seriously, his face stern. It was an hour later, and Elizabeth was seated across from Mr. Bowman's desk.

"I know, but—" Elizabeth began unhappily.

"An opinion is not a fact," Mr. Bowman continued, cutting her off.

"I know, but—"

"It's fine to get angry," Mr. Bowman said, *"but you must not let your personal feelings get in the way of your ability to report.* I thought you understood the importance of being objective."

"I do," Elizabeth cried. "It was a mistake that that those paragraphs got printed. I know it's hard to believe, but I meant to print a different version of that story."

"Well, don't make that mistake again," Mr. Bowman warned. "If you do, I may have to reconsider the wisdom of letting a student editor put out a newspaper without adult supervision. Dennis Cookman's father has already called me to complain about the story. And to top it off, it now seems that Mrs. Simmons was mistaken. The two boys who started the food fight in her shop were not Dennis and Alex. It was two boys from Big Mesa Middle School."

Elizabeth gasped.

"Mr. Clark called the principal of that school, and he confirmed that two of his students were seen causing trouble in Mrs. Simmons shop on the date in question. Mrs. Simmons mistook Dennis and Alex for those two boys. Dennis and Alex had no way of knowing what her concerns were. So naturally they were angry and upset when she refused to let them in. It was all a case of mistaken identity and poor communication."

"Oh, no!" Elizabeth cried.

"Oh, yes," Mr. Clark said. "You didn't go back to Dennis or Alex and ask them for their response to Mrs. Simmons's story. If you had, you might have uncovered the truth."

"I guess I just got so mad that . . ."

". . . that you didn't bother to check your facts," Mr. Bowman finished. "You made the same mistake that you made the first time."

"I'll print a correction in the next edition," Elizabeth promised. She shook her head ruefully. "Gosh, Mr. Bowman, at this rate there won't be anything in the paper except corrections and apologies."

Four

"Would you like to help Sweet Valley Middle School enlarge their soccer field?" Jessica asked hopefully. She held her collection can out to a young woman pushing a stroller.

Jessica and Elizabeth were on the third floor of the Sweet Valley Mall. Immediately after school the twins had come to the mall, along with lots of other kids. They all carried cans with Sweet Valley Middle School bumper stickers wrapped around them.

The lady smiled slightly and shook her head, passing Jessica, Elizabeth, and Lila without a backward glance.

Elizabeth sighed heavily. "This is terrible. We've been at the mall for an hour and we haven't collected a nickel."

"Would you please cheer up?" Jessica begged. "So you made a mistake on the newspaper. Big deal."

"Two mistakes," Elizabeth corrected. "And it *is* a big deal. If I goof up again, Mr. Bowman might not let me put out the paper on my own."

"Well, forget about it for now," Jessica said. "Let's get our minds on the soccer field."

"I can't get my mind off the apology I have to write to Dennis and Alex." Elizabeth sighed. "Maybe I'd better go on home. I'm sure not being much use here."

"Maybe we're just not going about this the right way," Jessica said. "People raise a lot of money for different causes by asking people for donations. There's no reason why we shouldn't be able to do it too. Maybe we're not being aggressive enough."

She spotted a friendly-looking lady heading in their direction. "Watch this," Jessica said confidently.

Jessica stepped into her path, and the lady smiled at her. "Excuse me," Jessica said quickly. "But we need your help to do something very important. You see, our boys' soccer team had a chance to play in Division A this year. But there's a problem."

The lady was watching Jessica's face intently and nodding, as if she was very interested in everything Jessica had to say.

Encouraged, Jessica plowed on. "The problem is

that our soccer field isn't regulation size. And it's going to cost five thousand dollars to enlarge it."

The lady nodded again, and Jessica began to feel certain that she had her donation.

"The school board says it doesn't have enough money to pay for the enlargement, so the kids at my school have decided to try to raise the money ourselves."

The lady smiled and lifted her eyebrows curiously.

"So I was wondering if you would like to donate some money to help us enlarge our soccer field."

Jessica paused, waiting for the lady to whip out her checkbook. But instead she frowned, as if she still wasn't quite sure what Jessica wanted from her.

"Any amount at all would help," Jessica added. "Whatever you feel like contributing."

The lady stared at Jessica for several seconds. Then she stared at Elizabeth. When neither girl said anything else, the lady gave them an apologetic smile. "I am sorry," she said with a heavy accent. "But I do not speak much English. If you are lost, perhaps you ask a policeman."

"Well, that was a washout," Elizabeth said with a sigh as the woman hurried away. "Maybe fund-raising just isn't our thing."

"Don't be so negative," Jessica cried. "So we hit a little language barrier. That doesn't mean we should give up. Come on," she said, grabbing

Elizabeth by the sleeve. "Let's try the second floor."

"My feet hurt," Elizabeth moaned an hour later. She sat down on one of the green wrought-iron benches that were scattered throughout the mall, and slid her feet out of her shoes. "Don't your feet hurt?"

"I guess so," Jessica muttered absently, glancing around the mall. "But I'd rather keep trying to raise money than sit."

"You're making me feel guilty," Elizabeth said with a smile. "You're really working hard at this."

"You bet," Jessica agreed, tapping her fingers impatiently against her can. "It's for an important cause."

"Hey! Look!" Jessica said suddenly in an eager voice.

Elizabeth's eyes followed Jessica's finger, which was pointing at an old man sitting on a bench on the other side of the mall.

"See that old man?" Jessica asked.

"Yeah."

"Look at what he's reading," Jessica said. "*National Sports Week* Magazine. I'll bet that means he's a real sports fan. Come on. Put your shoes on, and let's try him."

Elizabeth quickly slipped her loafers back on and followed Jessica over to the old man.

"Excuse me," Jessica said.

The old man lowered his magazine and stared

sternly at Jessica and Elizabeth from beneath his shaggy gray eyebrows. "Yes?"

"I see you're a sports fan," Jessica said.

"Ha!" the old man barked.

"What do you think that means?" Elizabeth asked under her breath as the man looked back down at his magazine.

"I don't know," Jessica whispered back. She took a deep breath and cleared her throat loudly until the man looked back up at them.

Jessica's face broke into a big smile, and she dug her elbow into Elizabeth's ribs. Elizabeth smiled as broadly as she could.

"Would you like to make a donation to help us raise five thousand dollars to enlarge the Sweet Valley Middle School soccer field to Division-A standards?" Jessica asked breathlessly, holding out her can.

The old man's brows knitted angrily. "No, I wouldn't," he retorted in a huffy tone. "Five thousand dollars, indeed." He waved his magazine under Jessica's nose. "Athletes today are spoiled. And so are kids. When I was your age, we didn't play fancy games like soccer. We played kick-the-can. And we didn't need a five-thousand-dollar field to play it on, either. All we needed was a tin can and a street."

The old man closed his magazine with a snap, making Jessica and Elizabeth jump. Then he stood up and glared. "Five thousand dollars!" the old man snorted again. "HA!" And with that he stomped angrily off in the direction of the shoe store.

"That's it," Elizabeth announced. "I'm going home."

"Don't give up yet. Maybe we'll have more luck with somebody closer to our own age," Jessica suggested. "They would understand why this is important. Ah ha!" she said happily. Walking in their direction was a boy who looked as if he was in sixth or seventh grade.

"Excuse me," Jessica said brightly. "But are you a soccer fan?"

"I sure am," the boy responded. "I'm on the Westpark Middle School soccer team."

"Really?" Jessica said cheerfully. "We go to Sweet Valley Middle School."

"I think we're scheduled to play you guys in a couple of months," the boy said. "We're really psyched. This is our first year in Division A."

"Ours, too," Jessica said. She put on a serious face. "But you may not get a chance to play us."

The boy frowned in confusion. "How come?"

"Because it turns out that our field isn't regulation size," Elizabeth explained.

"Bummer!" the boy said sympathetically.

"That's why we're here this afternoon," Jessica added. "We're trying to raise the five thousand dollars it will cost to enlarge the field to Division-A standards." She held out her can. "Would you like to make a contribution?"

"Sure," the boy said cheerfully. "Us kids have to help each other out." He dug into his pocket and produced a quarter. Then he dropped it in Jessica's can, where it landed with a happy *clank*.

"Thanks," Jessica said.

"*I'm* here because we're trying to repair some flood damage to our library." He held up his other hand, and Jessica realized that he was holding a can of his own. "Would *you* guys like to help *us*?"

Jessica gulped and exchanged a look with Elizabeth. She was tempted to say no, but the look in Elizabeth's eye made her think twice. They couldn't say no. Not after he had helped them. With a sinking heart, Jessica dug into the pocket of her jeans and found a quarter. So did Elizabeth.

Clank! went Jessica's quarter.

Clank! went Elizabeth's quarter.

"Thanks," the boy said happily, shaking the can so that the two quarters made a loud rattle. "Good luck. I'll look for you guys at the game."

"Bye," Jessica said.

"Bye," Elizabeth echoed softly.

"We haven't raised any money, and now we're down a quarter," Jessica said dejectedly after the boy had walked away.

"Looks like you guys aren't having much luck either," said a voice at Jessica's elbow.

Jessica looked over and saw that Amy Sutton, Maria Slater, and Ken Matthews had drifted over to join them.

"Hasn't anybody gotten anything?" Jessica asked.

Amy held up her can and shook it. The can didn't make a sound.

Maria shook her can, and Jessica heard a lone coin rattling around in it.

"Well, it's a start," Jessica said encouragingly.

"Not really," Maria answered mournfully. "Look." She held the can toward Jessica and the rest of the group. They all peered down and saw a button sitting in the bottom of the can.

Maria sighed. "A toddler gave it to me."

"Who are we kidding?" Ken said. "We'll never raise five thousand dollars in a week. It's a fortune. And besides, it's not important to anybody but us."

"But that's not true," Jessica protested.

"Yes, it is," Amy said. "This would be a lot easier if we could figure out some reason why people who don't go to Sweet Valley Middle School should care whether or not we have a soccer field."

"But people *should* care," Jessica protested.

"Why?" Amy asked.

Jessica frowned, thinking back to what Lois Lattimer had said. "The whole world would be better off if it stopped thinking *me*, and started thinking *we*," she said forcefully. "The students of Sweet Valley Middle School are the future of California. Why shouldn't people want to help us help ourselves? Doesn't everybody benefit if we grow up into healthy, athletic citizens? Citizens who learn how to play by the rules. Citizens who know how to compete." She paused dramatically and lifted her hands. "When you look at it that way, five thousand dollars isn't a lot of money. Not when you consider the return they'll get on their investment."

There was a loud burst of applause. When Jessica looked around, she noticed that several shoppers had gathered to listen to her speech.

"That was lovely," one lady said approvingly. She leaned over and dropped a five-dollar bill into Jessica's can.

"I'm a soccer fan myself," said another man. "And I know how much team sports meant to me when I was your age."

Clank! Clank! Clank! The man dropped a handful of change into Jessica's can.

"Thanks," she stammered, hardly able to believe the number of hands that were reaching out to drop green bills and silver change into their cans.

Within a few seconds the crowd had disbursed, and Elizabeth, Amy, Maria, and Ken gazed at Jessica in awe.

"That was a really great speech," Amy breathed. "Now I'm totally inspired." She shook her can, and it rattled merrily. "I see what you mean. This really is important."

Amy walked away, and Jessica watched her intercept a couple and begin talking eagerly. The couple's faces registered interest and approval. When

Amy held out her can, the man and the woman each produced a dollar bill and put it in Amy's can.

Amy turned toward the group and gave them a thumbs-up sign. The group around Jessica gave her a thumbs-up back.

"I'm going for it," Ken said, hurrying away to the other side of the mall.

Maria patted Jessica on the back. "You're a born activist," she said. "This really seems like a cause we can get behind. We're going to raise that five thousand dollars. And it'll all be thanks to you."

Five

Jessica hurried into the auditorium, feeling almost breathless with excitement. It was Thursday, the day Mr. Clark was going to announce the total of the collection campaign.

The last week had gone by in a blur. Between collecting money at the mall, giving speeches outside of shops, and encouraging other kids, Jessica had hardly had time even to talk to Aaron, or Randy, or Mr. Clark. She hadn't even had time for her friends. She'd spent her lunch hours doing the bare minimum of homework to keep up.

She had no idea how much money had been raised, but if everybody had worked even half as hard as she had, they were sure to have enough for the soccer field.

"Jessica!" she heard Aaron's voice call out as she entered the auditorium. "Over here."

Jessica saw Aaron sitting with Denny Jacobson, Peter Jefferies, and several other boys from the soccer team. They all waved at her. Aaron pointed to an empty seat next to him, and Jessica proudly hurried over to sit in it. Aaron smiled, and several of the boys said hello when Jessica sat down.

A little shiver of excitement ran up Jessica's spine when Mr. Clark stepped up to the microphone. She was almost certain that he was going to single her out for some special notice.

"First of all," Mr. Clark said as soon as the auditorium was quiet, "I want to congratulate all of you who worked so hard to raise money over the last week."

The auditorium burst into applause, and Jessica smiled proudly. Aaron squeezed her arm.

"Sweet Valley Middle School is going to have its soccer field," Mr. Clark announced.

"*Hooray!*" the audience shouted.

"One student in particular is responsible for this. I know you'll all want to join me in thanking that student."

Jessica swallowed the lump that was rising in her throat. It was incredibly moving. In a few moments Mr. Clark would ask her to stand up, and all the students would begin cheering for her.

"I'll bet he means you," Aaron whispered. "You were the biggest money raiser. Everybody knows how much time you spent at the mall."

Jessica lowered her eyes modestly. "I just did what anybody else would have done," she whispered.

"Thanks for working so hard," Aaron whispered. "I'm glad Mr. Clark is giving you credit."

"I don't care about getting credit," Jessica lied. "I'm just glad we're getting our soccer field."

Mr. Clark gave a big smile. "So let's have a big round of applause, for . . ."

Jessica began to get to her feet.

"Lila Fowler," Mr. Clark finished.

Lila!

Jessica fell back down into her seat and stared openmouthed with shock as Lila stepped shyly from the wings of the stage.

There was a roar of approval from the crowded auditorium, and Lila bobbed her head in acknowledgment.

"Unfortunately," Mr. Clark went on as soon as the applause died down, "the total amount collected by the students was only $1,767. But Mr. Fowler called me last night to tell me he would donate the balance of the money."

Mr. Clark produced a small package and removed something square-shaped and shiny. "When I learned of the Fowler family's generous gift, I called a local sign shop, who sprang into action. They prepared this plaque, and I think you will all agree with the sentiment expressed."

Mr. Clark pushed his glasses up on his nose and looked down at the plaque. "It reads . . . *To the Fowler family, from the students of Sweet Valley Middle School with gratitude. Without your generous support, this soccer field would not have been possible.*" He looked out again over the audience. "We'll attach this plaque to the first bleacher on the new soccer field."

Lila smiled modestly, and the whole audience burst into applause again.

"Thank you," she said in a breathy voice. She took the plaque from Mr. Clark, and her lip trembled a bit, as if she was too moved to speak for a moment. Then she swallowed and spoke tremulously into the microphone. "On behalf of my father, I would like to thank you all. I know he wishes he could be here today. When I told him about the soccer field and how important it was to all of us here at school, he wanted to help—especially when I told him how hard we had all worked to make our dream a reality." *We!* Jessica thought sourly. Lila had hardly worked at all. She'd stood sullenly around the mall for a couple of hours and then given up. Who was she kidding?

"I told my father it wasn't a donation," Lila said breathlessly. "I told him it was an investment. An investment in the future of the kids of Sweet Valley and the future of California."

She's not just stealing my credit, Jessica thought furiously. *She's stealing all my lines!*

There was another loud and enthusiastic burst of applause, and Lila smiled tearfully out across the audience.

"Wow. Lila's incredible, isn't she?" Aaron whispered happily. "How many girls could convince a grown-up that kids are worth investing in?"

Jessica ground her teeth. "Not many," she answered.

Peter Jefferies raised his hand.

"Peter," Mr. Clark said, spotting his hand. "Do you have something to say?"

Peter stood up. "I would like to officially express the boys' soccer team's thanks, and also say that all goals made in our first Division-A season will be dedicated to Lila Fowler."

Lila burst into a broad grin, and the audience applauded again.

Everyone but Jessica. She couldn't believe it. Couldn't believe that after all her hard work, and planning, and dedication, Lila had snatched all the glory. It just wasn't fair.

"Thank you," Lila said, flashing another huge smile.

"I'd also like to ask Lila to serve as my honorary co-captain," Peter added.

There was another burst of happy applause, and even Mr. Clark joined in. He leaned back toward the microphone. "I think that's all, then," he said. "You're dismissed."

"Lila is amazing. Can you imagine being able to

talk a grown-up into giving that much money?" Ken said.

"I never realized how important someone like Lila can be to a school," Jessica heard Winston Egbert say.

Lila was coming down off the stage, and kids were rushing in her direction.

"Ouch!" Jessica cried as Aaron and the other boys practically knocked her down in their hurry to get to Lila.

Jessica watched Lila get mobbed. She couldn't stand it. It wasn't fair. It wasn't fair at all.

Suddenly, hot tears began to sting her eyes. She turned and raced out the side door, practically knocking Coach Cassels over in her hurry. "Sorry," she muttered.

But Coach Cassels didn't even seem to notice that Jessica had bumped into him. Just like everybody else, he was in too much of a hurry to get to Lila to notice Jessica at all.

"Jessica!" Elizabeth shouted, spotting Jessica by her locker. "Wait up. I looked all over for you after the assembly," Elizabeth panted as she hurried over to join her. "But you must have left the auditorium as soon as it was over."

"Sure I did," Jessica said dryly. "I didn't know anybody would be looking for *me*." She shoved a book into her locker and removed some notebooks.

Elizabeth frowned. "I wanted to get a quote

from you for *The Sixers*. The soccer field is big news."

"No comment," Jessica said sourly.

"No comment?" Elizabeth repeated. "What's the matter with you? I thought you would be thrilled."

"Well, I'm not," Jessica said, yanking some books and papers out of her locker and shutting it with a bang. "Why should I be happy about it?" she demanded angrily. "It doesn't have anything to do with me."

"What do you mean?" Elizabeth asked.

"I did lots more work than Lila," Jessica said, her voice wobbling. "I'm the one who cared. I'm the one who convinced people to give money. I'm the one who did everything. And now Lila's getting all the credit."

"Jessica!" Elizabeth cried. "I'm ashamed of you. I thought you had changed over the last few days. I thought you were more interested in building a soccer field than in competing with Lila."

"I'm *not* competing with Lila," Jessica argued. "Don't you see? She's competing with *me*."

Just then Elizabeth and Jessica looked up and saw Lila coming down the hall. All around her, kids were talking and laughing and slapping her on the back.

As Elizabeth watched, Lila met Jessica's stare and gave her a little sneer. Then she turned and whispered something to Janet, and they both laughed nastily.

As the group passed by, Lila leaned toward Jessica. "Not jealous, are you?" she hissed.

Elizabeth's mouth fell open in shock. Lila really was being pretty awful.

"Hey, Lila!" Peter Jefferies said. "After school, let's all get together on the soccer field. Since you're honorary co-captain of the team, you'll want to see some of the plays we're working on."

"See what I mean?" Jessica said with a sigh as the group went down the hall. "She did it just to show me up. To make me jealous."

Elizabeth put her hand on Jessica's shoulder. "I'm really sorry, Jess. I know you worked hard. And *The Sixers* is going to make sure everybody knows it."

I hate Lila, Jessica thought.

It was late afternoon, and Jessica sat alone in the woods behind the soccer field, watching the boys' team show the Unicorns some of their fancy plays.

I hate the Unicorns, too, Jessica thought. None of them had asked her to join them. In fact, Janet and Lila had made a point of excluding her when the group had headed for the soccer field after school.

"Another point for me," she heard Aaron shout as he kicked the ball across the goal line. "I dedicate this goal to Lila, without whose generous support our soon-to-be-built soccer field would not have been possible," he said in a deep, official-sounding voice.

The laughter of the group floated toward Jessica, who was hidden from view by the some low-hanging branches.

Most of all, she thought, *I hate soccer.*

A tear began to trickle down her cheek, and she rested her head against the thick trunk of one of the shady trees. She'd never felt so abandoned, friendless, and unappreciated in her life.

"It's not fair," she said. "It's not fair at all."

A breeze ruffled the treetops, and the leaves made a soothing, rustling sound as Jessica bowed her head and cried. Then a soft cheeping sound above her got her attention. She lifted her teary eyes and saw a small brown bird perched on the lowest limb of the tree. He cocked his head sideways and studied Jessica intently.

"If you're going to tell me the important thing is that the school got the soccer field, please don't," Jessica said sarcastically, and sniffled.

The little bird hopped closer, then cocked his head again, giving her a curious look.

"I guess you're wondering what I'm doing out here, crying by myself."

The bird let out a low, throaty "chirrup."

"I'm out here crying by myself because all my friends are horrible," Jessica choked. "And because nobody cares about me." The bird began to hop around, and Jessica almost had to smile. It seemed as if he understood what she was saying. He began to flutter his wings angrily and let out a series of indignant squeaks.

Jessica was touched. "Thank you for your support," she whispered, expecting him to fly away any second.

But instead he hopped farther down the branch and settled himself almost within arm's reach.

Jessica leaned back against the comfortingly thick trunk of the tree and began crying harder, grateful for the trees that surrounded her and shielded her from view, and for the company of the tiny brown bird.

Six

Elizabeth held up her camera. "Smile," she instructed Lila.

Lila posed in front of the lockers and proudly turned up the collar of the soccer jacket she was wearing. Elizabeth focused the camera and snapped the picture. Behind Elizabeth, all the other Unicorns sighed happily.

"That jacket looks fantastic on you," Mandy Miller said.

"I wish I had one," Tamara Chase commented enviously.

"You're really doing great things for the Unicorns' image," Janet said approvingly.

"Oh, it was nothing," Lila said modestly, rolling up the sleeves of the jacket. The boys had presented it to her right after first period that morning, and she hadn't taken it off since.

It was Friday afternoon, and Mr. Clark had suggested to Elizabeth that morning that it might be nice to put Lila's picture on the front page of *The Sixers*, posing with her father. Lila had called her father, and he had agreed. But later he had called the school to say that he had an important business meeting and they should just take a picture of Lila by herself.

"Is Lila's picture going to be the only one in the paper?" Janet asked.

Elizabeth nodded. "Uh-huh. There's room for only one picture in the issue. It's too bad we don't have room for a picture of everybody who worked hard to raise the money, but I'm definitely going to mention everybody's name," she said forcefully.

"Hey, Lila!" Peter called out from the other end of the hall. "Want to come to Casey's with the team to get some ice cream?"

"Sure." Lila smiled and turned to the other Unicorns. "Why don't we all go?"

There were a lot of excited giggles and whispers as the Unicorns hurried behind Lila to join Peter and the other boys.

Elizabeth turned to put her camera back in the case and saw Jessica standing by herself behind a row of lockers. The look on her face made Elizabeth feel just awful for her. Elizabeth knew that Jessica really had worked hard to raise the money for the soccer field, and she had been counting on getting her name and picture in the paper.

And now the whole school was fawning over Lila and ignoring Jessica completely.

"Please don't feel so bad," Elizabeth begged.

"I don't care," Jessica muttered.

But Elizabeth knew that she did. Jessica had spent almost the entire evening yesterday brooding in her room. Elizabeth couldn't blame her for feeling bad. It wasn't fair that Lila was getting so much glory and being the center of attention. Jessica sighed heavily and shoved her books into her locker. "Ready to go home?"

"Not yet," Elizabeth answered. "I'm going to conduct an interview for the next edition of *The Sixers*."

"An interview with Lila?" Jessica asked sadly. "You'll have to go to Casey's."

Elizabeth laughed. "What makes you think I'm interviewing Lila?"

"Because you're just as bad as everybody else," Jessica retorted. "You know I worked a hundred times harder than Lila to raise money, but you're putting her picture on the front page of the newspaper instead of mine."

Elizabeth sighed. She'd been expecting this. "Jessica! Donating that much money to the school is front-page news."

"Oh, sure," Jessica said sarcastically, shutting her locker with a bang. "You told me *The Sixers* was going to make sure everybody knew how hard I worked."

"I'm going to put your name in the paper," Elizabeth insisted.

"Big deal," Jessica said. "My name will be in a great big thick paragraph along with a hundred other kids' names. I can't believe you're stabbing me in the back like this. I'm your *sister*."

"Being my sister has nothing to do with it," Elizabeth argued. "News is news. Putting Lila on the front page was a purely objective decision."

Jessica sighed unhappily. "You're my sister. You're not supposed to be objective."

"I'm a newspaper editor, too. And I've learned my lesson. I have to be objective, no matter what my personal feelings are." Elizabeth's face softened. "Come with me to my interview," she suggested. "I'm talking to the engineer who's going to enlarge the soccer field."

"No, thanks," Jessica said. "I don't think I want to hear any more about the soccer field. Ever. That's the last time I take up a cause." She gave the wall a moody kick with her toe.

"Well, it's the last time you should take up a cause just to get glory," Elizabeth retorted, losing her patience. "Causes are about getting something accomplished. You should feel happy about the soccer field, not angry because you're not famous for it."

"Well, I am," Jessica said, her face clouding over.

Elizabeth sighed. "Try to forget about it, would you?" she pleaded. "Come with me to the interview. It'll be interesting to see the plans. It's better than walking home by yourself and spending the rest of the day in your room."

"Oh, OK," Jessica agreed reluctantly.

Elizabeth patted Jessica on the shoulder. "That's the spirit."

"The problem with enlarging the field," the engineer said, illustrating her point with her hands, "is that in order to enlarge it to the proper size and keep the shape, it's got to be enlarged on two sides."

Elizabeth nodded and scribbled quickly as the engineer spoke.

I hate that soccer field, Jessica thought. *I hate it. I hate it. I hate it.*

"As you can see," the engineer went on, pointing to the far side of the field, "if we try to expand in that direction, we run into the tennis courts. To move the courts would add another several thousand dollars onto the cost of the work. So what we'll do is expand the field in the other direction."

She pointed to the woods that bordered the field on the far side. "We'll bulldoze some of the trees over there, and that will give us room to enlarge the field and build the new bleachers."

"Bulldoze the trees!" Elizabeth and Jessica both cried out at the same time.

The engineer smiled, and her eyes crinkled at the corners. "We won't be bulldozing all the trees," she assured them. "Just the ones that line the perimeter of the field. It's the most efficient way to get the job done."

Jessica squinted at the thick grove of trees that lined the soccer field, remembering how they had sheltered her the day before, when she had been so upset. They felt like old friends. In fact, they felt like her only friends. She would be sorry to see them go.

I hate the soccer field, Jessica thought again. *I just hate it.*

"So they're going to bulldoze some of the trees," Mr. Wakefield said thoughtfully that night at the dinner table. "That's a shame. When I was a kid, I loved roaming through those woods. We used to camp there, play hide-and-seek, and roam for hours. Most of what I learned about nature, I learned in those woods."

"I didn't know those woods were there when you were a kid," Steven said, shoving a forkful of mashed potatoes in his mouth.

"Those trees were around when my dad was a kid," Mr. Wakefield responded.

"Lois Lattimer says old trees are a national treasure," Steven said. "She was talking about it on a talk show recently."

"Well," Mr. Wakefield said, "I guess it all depends on how old is old, relatively speaking."

"How old are the trees around the school?" Elizabeth asked.

"I don't know," Mr. Wakefield said. "But it might be interesting to find out."

"I think I will try to find out," Elizabeth said. "It would be interesting to include that information in the article about the construction. How could I find out about it?"

"Try the Nature Society," Mrs. Wakefield suggested. "They have a lot of experts on staff over there. It would be an interesting field trip for you."

Elizabeth watched Jessica listlessly push the food around on her plate. Jessica was still way down in the dumps over Lila and the soccer field. Maybe if she could get Jessica interested in finding out about the trees, it would take her mind off of her troubles. "Why don't you come too," Elizabeth said to Jessica.

"Yes, Jessica," Mrs. Wakefield urged. "Why don't you go with Elizabeth? You've always been interested in nature."

"She has?" Steven asked.

"I have?" Jessica echoed, looking up with a surprised face. "Sure," Mrs. Wakefield said. "After all, you were the one who found that baby seal that had been caught in the oil spill. You took it to the aquarium and nursed it back to health."

"Yeah, but she just did that because she had a crush on the guy who worked there," Steven added with a laugh.

"That was true at first," Jessica said hotly. "But then I really did care about Whiskers."

"Stop arguing," Mr. Wakefield said. "It doesn't matter why somebody does something good. All that matters is that they do it. If you started examining everybody's motives for doing good in the world, you wouldn't like what you saw, and nothing good would ever get done."

"So will you come?" Elizabeth asked Jessica.

Jessica shrugged. "Sure. It's not like anybody else is asking me to do anything."

Seven

"I'm really glad you decided to come with me," Elizabeth said the next morning as the girls rode their bicycles toward the Sweet Valley Nature Society. "I know you're really down over the soccer field. But sometimes if you take an interest in something besides your own problems, it makes you feel better."

Jessica rolled her eyes and sighed. She wished Elizabeth hadn't dragged her along today. She didn't want to take an interest in something besides her own problems. All she wanted to do was sit in her room and think about how much she hated Lila and Janet and Aaron and the soccer field and everybody at school who was ignoring her and gushing over Lila.

"Are you going to sulk forever?" Elizabeth demanded impatiently when Jessica didn't answer.

"Sorry," Jessica mumbled as they pulled up in the front of the low brick building that stood in front of the four-acre arboretum and animal refuge. They hopped off their bikes, locked them to the bike rack, and went inside.

"Wow!" Elizabeth said. "Look at all this stuff."

All around the lobby were posters of birds, elephants, and rhinos. There were also little dioramas that showed rain forests, wetlands, and animal scenes. "I could spend all day in here," Elizabeth said happily.

"May I help you?"

Elizabeth and Jessica looked up and saw a tall, nice-looking man with a beard smiling at them. Jessica did a double take when she noticed the bird in his hand. It looked just like the birds that nested in the woods behind Sweet Valley Middle School. Just like the bird that had kept her company when she was feeling so alone.

"Hi," Elizabeth said. "My name is Elizabeth Wakefield, and this is my sister, Jessica."

"How do you do?" the man said politely. "My name is Bill Watkins, and my friend here is called Tweeter."

Jessica couldn't take her eyes off the little brown bird. It sat so still and watchful in the palm of Bill's hand. "Is he a pet?" Jessica asked.

"Yes and no," Bill said. "He lived in some woods about forty miles from here that were cut down.

One of the loggers found Tweeter on the ground when he was just a tiny chick. The logger figured Tweeter must have been in the nest when the tree came down."

"Where was Tweeter's mother?" Jessica asked.

Bill shrugged. "I guess she flew away when they started cutting down the trees." He held his hand out to Jessica and let her stroke Tweeter's little head. "We raised him, and he's been here ever since. We've tried to turn him loose, but he always flies back. I guess he can't find any place he fits in anymore." Jessica felt a tear sting the corner of her eye. She knew exactly how Tweeter felt.

It was awful that the little bird's home was lost. There were tons of birds in the woods behind Sweet Valley Middle School. Would lots of them be left homeless too? Jessica wished she hadn't come. This wasn't making her feel better. It was making her feel worse.

"Was there something I could do for you girls?" Bill asked.

"We go to Sweet Valley Middle School, and I'm the editor of the sixth-grade paper," Elizabeth explained. "Our school is going to expand our soccer field. To do that, they're going to have to cut down part of the woods that are around the existing field. My dad was saying that some of the trees are really old. I thought it would be nice to do a little article on them. Sort of like an elegy."

"There are a lot of old trees in this part of

California," Bill agreed. "In fact, there are trees around Sweet Valley that are almost four hundred years old."

"Four hundred years old!" Elizabeth exclaimed. "That's really old."

Jessica knitted her brows. "People are always worrying about saving really old trees, right?"

"That's right," Bill said. "This may not be what you want to hear, but if the trees are that old, the construction really should be challenged."

"If the construction is challenged," Elizabeth said, "that would hold up the expansion of the soccer field."

"It might stop the expansion altogether," Bill agreed. "Preserving trees is a pretty important issue these days."

Jessica looked down at the little bird in Bill's hand. The bird met her stare with an unblinking, trusting gaze.

"Maybe the construction *should* be stopped," Jessica said thoughtfully. "Maybe the Nature Society should do something."

Bill laughed. "The Nature Society's got a pretty big list of projects right now."

"But birds like Tweeter are going to lose their homes," Jessica argued. "You can't stand back and let that happen." She banged her fist down on the counter. "You *have* to do something about it," she cried. "You just have to."

Bill laughed and held up his free hand. "Hold

on there, Lois Lattimer," he said in a teasing tone. "It's no good to demand that people do what they don't have the time or resources to do. All of our money, time, and energy is already committed."

"But the woods around our school are special," Jessica protested. "At least they are to me. And to my dad, too."

Bill smiled and put his hand on Jessica's shoulder. "Everybody thinks their patch of earth is the most beautiful and the most special. And if you really believe that, you have to work to save it yourself. Problems get solved when people at the local level get involved and work together toward a solution."

A lady stepped into the lobby from the inner office. "Bill," she said, "our staff meeting is about to start."

"I've got to get back to work," Bill said. He smiled at Elizabeth. "Help yourself to our information packets," he added, nodding toward the stack of shiny pamphlets that lay on the reception desk. "They should give you lots of good information for your article."

"Thanks," Elizabeth said, taking three or four of them from the stack.

"Call me if you need anything else for your article." He smiled at Jessica. "And you let me know what happens to the trees," he said. Then he turned, and he and Tweeter disappeared into the inner office.

*   *   *

Elizabeth quickly unlocked her bicycle and put her books in the basket. If she hurried, maybe she could get on her bike and start pedaling before Jessica had a chance to say anything like—

"So," she heard Jessica say, practically echoing the words that were in Elizabeth's mind. "I certainly hope your article on the trees is going to demand that the construction be canceled."

"Arghhh!" Elizabeth groaned with a sinking heart. "I knew you were going to say that. I just *knew* you were going to say that."

"Well, you *have* to," Jessica insisted. "You heard what Bill Watkins said. Do you want to see old trees bulldozed?"

Elizabeth stamped her foot. "The minute he said that about the trees I knew you were going to start some kind of thing about it. You had that look in your eye."

"What look in my eye?"

"The look that tells me to watch out, because my life is getting ready to turn upside down. The look that says I'm going to wind up involved in something I'll regret. The look that tells me to run for my life."

"Lizzie!" Jessica cried. "Quit babbling about my eye and start thinking about those trees. You can't just sit around while they tear them down."

"It *is* a shame," Elizabeth said reasonably. "But there will still be lots of trees left."

"But what about the birds and squirrels who live in those trees?" Jessica cried.

"They'll go and live in the other trees," Elizabeth answered.

"How can you be so heartless!" Jessica exclaimed, her voice breaking a little. "I can't believe you're not determined to save those trees."

"I think you're being a little overemotional," Elizabeth said.

"At least I care," Jessica retorted.

"I care too," Elizabeth said.

"If you really cared, you would write an article saying how terrible it is to cut down the trees. You're a reporter."

"A reporter's job is to report," Elizabeth said, quoting Mr. Bowman. "To present facts and be objective."

Jessica put her hands on her hips. "Well, an activist's job is to get active. And that's what I'm going to do. If I do something to bring people's attention to this, you'd *have* to report it, wouldn't you?"

Elizabeth stamped her foot again. "I'm working very hard to make *The Sixers* a serious newspaper. I'm not going to let you use me—or it—just to get attention for yourself."

"I'm not just trying to get attention for myself," Jessica protested angrily. "I'm doing it to get attention for my cause."

"I thought you said you were through with

causes!" Elizabeth shouted in frustration.

"I'm through with causes that help *people*," Jessica shouted back. "People are mean and selfish. But trees and animals are helpless and nice."

"So that's it," Elizabeth said, crossing her arms over her chest. "You're doing this for revenge. You're just trying to stop the soccer field to get back at Lila."

"I'm trying to stop the soccer field because it's the right thing to do," Jessica insisted.

Elizabeth sighed. "Well, I guess if you're determined to go ahead with this, I can't stop you. Like Dad said, your motives aren't important. What's important is doing something good. I just wish I knew whether or not this was good."

"Tweeter would think it was good," Jessica said decisively. "And that's good enough for me."

Eight

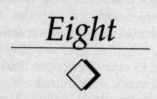

"Four hundred years old," Mandy Miller exclaimed, standing beside Jessica's locker. "Gosh, that's really old. That's really, really old."

"Exactly," Jessica said. "And trees that old are a national treasure."

"National treasures should be protected," Mandy added. "It's not right to cut them down."

"I agree," Amy Sutton said thoughtfully. "It's not right to destroy something that old."

"I can't stop worrying about all the little animals," Sarah Thomas said. "It's terrible to think they would lose their homes."

"I knew you guys would see it like that," Jessica said.

It was before homeroom on Monday, and Jessica had gotten to school early to tell Amy, Mandy, and

Sarah what she'd learned at the Nature Society. Just as she had expected, all three girls agreed with her wholeheartedly.

Amy was more Elizabeth's friend than Jessica's, but Jessica knew Amy had some very definite ideas about the environment.

Mandy was a committed conservationist too. She recycled everything, and she was always urging the other Unicorns to save their bottles, cans, and paper.

Sarah was crazy about animals. Jessica knew the Thomases' garage was usually full of stray dogs and birds with broken wings. Sarah was always finding animals that needed help and nursing them back to health.

"What can we do about it?" Amy asked.

"Start a SAVE THE TREES campaign," Jessica said. "Get everyone at school involved in saving the trees. If everybody supports it, then Mr. Clark would have to stop the construction."

"Good idea," Mandy said. "We've got to try to save them."

"No," Jessica corrected. "We've got to *succeed* in saving them."

"The first step is to make everybody aware of what's going on," Amy said.

"How?" Mandy asked.

"I know," Sarah said, beckoning the girls to follow her. She led them down the hall and into the empty art room that was used to store supplies. "We can make some posters," she said. "We can start now and finish them at lunch. We'll hang them all over school."

"Great idea," Jessica said happily. Sarah was a very talented artist. She'd done posters for lots of school projects, and her drawings were always very realistic.

"You guys make the posters," Mandy said, her eyes sparkling with enthusiasm. "I'll make some leaflets to hand out at lunch. I can use the photocopier in the secretary's office."

"Good idea," Amy said. "I'll help you."

Mandy and Amy hurried away, and Sarah reached for some sheets of paper.

Jessica grabbed some pots of paint. "We're going to have to work fast," she said. "Mr. Clark's secretary said the bulldozer is scheduled to come on Friday morning."

Sarah's face took on a determined look. "We'll work fast, all right. And we'll work hard, too. This is a good thing that you're doing. I think people will really get behind us."

"Save the trees!" Jessica shouted. *"Save the trees!"*

She was standing in the hall in front of a big poster with a tree painted on it. Perched at the top of the tree was a little bird in a nest. SAVE THE TREES was emblazoned across the top of the poster. Jessica and Sarah had painted twenty of them and hung them on every available wall of the school.

Mandy and Amy had made leaflets explaining how the construction was going to destroy valuable trees that were four hundred years old, and how thousands of birds and squirrels would be left homeless.

Now Jessica was handing them out to raise people's consciousness.

"*Save the trees!*" Jessica shouted, thrusting a leaflet into Lloyd Benson's hand as he came hurrying by on his way to class.

Lloyd stared down at it. "What's this all about?" he asked.

"It's about saving important trees," Jessica answered.

Lloyd scanned the leaflet, and his bfow furrowed. "Wow, this is terrible. I had no idea those trees were that old. We don't have any right to cut them down just so we can have a soccer field."

"That's right," Jessica agreed. "And we need everybody to get involved to stop it."

"We sure do," Lloyd said. "I'm just trying to think what I can do to help. Hey, I know! I'll start a petition."

"That's a great idea," Jessica said enthusiastically.

"I'll write it tonight," Lloyd said eagerly. "And I'll start collecting signatures in the cafeteria during lunch period tomorrow."

Lloyd happily hurried off, then stopped. He turned. "Hey, Jessica."

"Yeah?"

"I think it's really great that you're doing this. Saving trees is really important."

"Thanks," Jessica said, her cheeks flushing pink with pride. *"Save the trees!"* she shouted louder. *"Save the trees!"*

"What trees?" Peter Burns asked as he strolled by.

"The trees that are going to be destroyed by the new soccer field," Jessica answered, handing him a leaflet.

Peter's eyes opened wide. "This is horrible. I like soccer and everything, but I like the environment more."

"Great," Jessica said. "Then will you sign the petition that Lloyd Benson is writing?"

"I'll do more than that," Peter said. "I'll help you guys organize a protest. I'll ask my dad how to do it. He was a political activist in the sixties. I'll bet he'll give me lots of good advice."

"That would be great," Jessica said happily.

"My dad is always complaining about how kids today don't get involved. He'll be really glad to hear about you and your SAVE THE TREES campaign."

The admiration in his eyes was unmistakable, and Jessica felt a surge of pride. Getting involved in something larger than herself, larger than the Unicorns, and even larger than Sweet Valley Middle School, was more exciting than she had ever dreamed.

"*Save the trees!*" Jessica shouted as Peter hurried away. "*Save the trees!*"

"What are you shouting about?" she heard a voice ask behind her. Jessica whirled around and saw Aaron giving her a friendly smile.

She handed him a leaflet. "This. I'm trying to make people aware of the importance of saving the trees behind the school."

Aaron scratched his head as he read the leaflet. "But according to this, if we don't cut down the trees, we won't have a soccer field."

"That's true," Jessica admitted. "But aren't the trees more important than soccer?"

Aaron's eyebrows shot up to his hairline. "Not to me," he said. "I think soccer is pretty important. There are trees all over the place. What we need is a new soccer field."

"Don't be so selfish," Jessica said angrily. "You're on the soccer team, so you think soccer is more important than trees. But if you were a bird, you'd feel differently."

Aaron balled the leaflet up angrily in his fist. "This is crazy, Jessica. I can't believe you're really going to try to stop the soccer field."

"If you don't believe it," Jessica said, "read my lips. Save the trees," she shouted again. "*Save the trees!*"

Aaron's mouth tightened angrily. He threw the balled-up leaflet in the trash can and stalked away.

*   *   *

"OK," Mandy said, rolling up a fresh batch of posters the following afternoon. "I'll take these and tack them up in the—" Mandy broke off when she saw Janet, Lila, Mary Wallace, Tamara Chase, Grace Oliver, Kimberly Haver, and Betsy Gordon file into the empty art room that the SAVE THE TREES campaign had turned into their headquarters.

Janet didn't look too friendly. Lila looked absolutely furious.

"Hi," Jessica said warily. "Have you come to help?"

"No," Janet snapped. "We haven't come to help. This is an emergency meeting of the Unicorn Club. As president of the Unicorns, I've come to demand that you two stop this SAVE THE TREES campaign right now."

"Jessica is just doing it to be obnoxious," Lila said to Mandy. "She's trying to spoil things because the plaque on the soccer field is going to read 'with thanks to the Fowler family' instead of 'with thanks to Jessica Wakefield.' She's only doing it because she's jealous."

"That's not true," Jessica insisted.

"Well, all I know is that nobody would go to that much trouble just to save a few moldy old trees," Lila said with a sniff.

"I would," Mandy said.

"So would I," Mary said quietly.

Janet whirled on Mary. "What do you mean by that?"

Mary frowned. "Even if Jessica is doing this to get back at Lila, it doesn't change the fact that the trees are four hundred years old, and we should be fighting to preserve them."

Janet put her hands on her hips. "I'm surprised at you, Mary. Where's your Unicorn spirit?"

Mary looked down at her feet, and several of the girls shifted uncomfortably.

Janet tapped her foot. "OK, everybody. We're all Unicorns, and we may have our differences and competitions. But sometimes we have to put our differences aside for the good of the club." Her face darkened. "Anybody who can't do that might want to think about joining some other club, as of now."

"What are you saying?" Mandy demanded, narrowing her eyes.

Janet stared back at her through steely eyes. "I'm saying that it's the trees or the Unicorns. Take your pick."

All the girls sucked in their breaths in shocked surprise. "Janet," Kimberly breathed, "don't you think that's a little drastic?"

Mandy lifted her chin. "I pick the trees," she said defiantly.

Jessica's heart was thudding so hard she felt almost sick. Was she really prepared to drop out of the most prestigious club of girls in Sweet Valley—over a cause?

For a second she considered throwing down the posters and apologizing to Lila. Making up with

Janet. Laughing with the Unicorns over this ridiculous argument and catching up on all the latest gossip.

But then she pictured Tweeter sitting in the palm of Bill Watkins's hand. She remembered sitting in the woods, feeling alone and unhappy. The Unicorns hadn't been there for her then. The trees had.

"I pick the trees too," Jessica said firmly.

"Me, too," Mary whispered.

"Mary!" Grace and Kimberly and Tamara all exclaimed. "No!"

"Yes," Mary said. She hurried past Janet and over to Jessica's side. "I'm sorry," she said, her voice practically whispering. "But I have to do what's right."

"Jessica Wakefield, you are mean, selfish, and stupid," Janet spat.

"And you're selfish and childish and—and stupid too," Jessica shot back bitterly. "I can't believe we were ever even friends."

"This is war, Jessica," Janet warned. And with that, she turned and stalked out, with Lila and the remaining Unicorns following behind her.

"Geez," Mary said nervously. "I hope I made the right decision."

Jessica realized that both Mary and Mandy were looking at her with wide, uncertain eyes.

They'd both given up a lot for this cause, and it was obvious that they were beginning to wonder if it was worth it.

Jessica lifted her chin. It was going to take strong leadership to keep everybody committed. She was going to make sure they got it.

"You made the right decision," she said in the most confident voice she could manage. "Trust me."

Nine

"*Save the trees!*" the crowd of students shouted as they marched behind Jessica on Wednesday morning before school. "*Save the trees.*"

Elizabeth sat on the school wall several yards away and watched her sister lead the protesters as they marched back and forth past the front doors of Sweet Valley Middle School.

"Pretty amazing, huh?" Todd Wilkins said, sitting down next to her. "Until yesterday morning, nobody had ever even given those trees a second thought. Now all of a sudden they're a big issue."

Elizabeth nodded. "People do seem to be getting pretty excited about them."

"Yeah. And lots of people are just as excited about the soccer field," Todd said. "I heard there's going to be a counterdemonstration."

"Really?" Elizabeth asked.

"Yeah. The SAVE THE SOCCER FIELD faction is meeting in the school auditorium right now."

Elizabeth pulled her reporter's notebook out of her backpack. "Well," she said, "in the interests of fair reporting, I think I'd better check it out."

"There are hundreds of trees in the woods behind the soccer field," Peter Jefferies was saying to the large group of students assembled in the auditorium. "To block the construction of the new soccer field just to save a few of them is totally ridiculous."

"Yeah!!" shouted the crowed.

"We've got to fight back!" Peter said, pounding his fist on the podium. "The majority of students in this school want a soccer field. We're going to get our soccer field!"

"Yeah!!!!" the crowd shouted again. There was lots of whistling and applause.

Elizabeth was scribbling as fast as she could, trying to take down Peter's words and capture the feeling of electric excitement that was racing through the auditorium.

It was terrible to see people getting upset and angry with each other—but on the other hand, it was exciting to see people so involved in their causes.

"What did you find out?" Todd asked when

Elizabeth came back outside a few minutes later and sat down on the wall.

"I found out the other side cares a lot about the soccer field," Elizabeth said with a smile. "And they're going to fight for it."

"Save the soccer field!" she heard someone shout in the distance.

Elizabeth and Todd both looked up and saw a crowd of students coming around the corner of the building. Lila, Aaron, and Peter were marching side by side in front of a big line of people. They were carrying signs that said "SAVE THE SOCCER FIELD."

As the line got closer, the SAVE THE TREES group began to shout louder. *"Save the trees!"* they yelled. *"Save the trees!"*

The crowd of soccer-field demonstrators formed a line along the front of the school that ran parallel to the line of the SAVE THE TREES demonstrators. *"Save the soccer field!"* they all shouted together. There were at least as many people on the pro-soccer side as there were on the pro-tree side. Aside from Peter Jefferies, Aaron, Denny, and several of the Unicorns, Elizabeth spotted Charlie Cashman and Bruce Patman from the soccer team.

"Tree killers!" Sophia Rizzo shouted accusingly. She stepped out of the pro-tree line and pointed angrily at Peter. "Tree killers!"

Elizabeth shook her head. Sophia was a good friend of hers, and usually she was really sensible and smart. But at that moment she looked hot-headed and irrational.

"Tree huggers!" Peter shouted in retaliation.

There was a loud burst of laughter, and then everyone on the pro-soccer side began to chant. "Tree huggers! Tree huggers! Tree huggers!" they taunted.

Elizabeth chewed unhappily on her thumbnail. Taking a position and demonstrating was one thing. Calling each other names was something else. Did Sophia really think she would change anybody's mind by calling them a "tree killer"?

And did Peter actually think he would solve anything by calling Sophia a "tree hugger"?

It was funny, but all the controversy that had seemed exciting a few minutes ago was beginning to feel mean-spirited and a little scary.

"Tree killers! Tree killers!" Jessica's side shouted.

"You people are just jealous because you didn't make the team!" Charlie shouted.

"Oh, yeah?" Belinda Layton shouted back, step-ping forward from the pro-tree line. "I made the girls' team, but I'd rather save the trees than play some stupid game."

A wadded-up leaflet came flying through the air and . . .

Smack!

. . . hit Belinda squarely on the forehead.

"Hey!" she protested. Immediately she retrieved the wad of paper and lobbed it back in the direction of the pro-soccer crowd, where it bounced off of Janet's shoulder.

It seemed to be the signal that everyone was waiting for, because the next thing Elizabeth knew, wads of paper were flying back and forth across the two lines. People were shouting names and insults at the top of their voices.

"Stop it!" an angry voice thundered over the din. *"Stop it right now, or you're all suspended!"*

The crowd of angry students suddenly fell silent at the sound of Mr. Clark's voice. He stood on the front steps of the school, holding a clipboard and a pen. "Now listen to me!" he shouted. "I understand that there is some disagreement over the construction of the soccer field. But I will not stand for this kind of disorderly conduct from either side. I am fully prepared to listen to both sides of the argument—in my office."

"Two, four, six, eight! We will not negotiate!" Jessica shouted angrily.

Mr. Clark put his hand on his hips. *"What was that?"* he demanded.

Jessica stepped forward. "We don't want to discuss anything. We demand that you cancel the construction of the soccer field—*now!*"

Elizabeth sucked in her breath with a gasp. Jessica wasn't going to help her cause by being rude to Mr. Clark.

"Miss Wakefield," Mr. Clark said in a patient but seething tone, "if you ever use that tone of voice again with me, I will call your parents down here and the four of us will have a long talk about courtesy. That goes for everyone in this school. Do I make myself clear?"

Jessica's cheeks flushed red, and her mouth closed in a sullen line. "Yes, sir," she muttered.

The bell rang, and Mr. Clark clapped his hands. "I want everyone to take a deep breath, get ahold of their tempers, and go to class."

"Yes, sir," several people said softly.

"Wow," Todd said, letting out his breath. "What a mess."

Elizabeth nodded. "You're right. It is a mess."

"I guess you're on Jessica's side," Todd said.

"I'm not on anybody's side," Elizabeth said quickly. "I'm a reporter. I'm completely objective."

Todd looked skeptical. "My mom says newspapers are never *completely* objective."

"Well, maybe they don't always succeed in being objective," Elizabeth retorted. "But they try."

"How can you help but be pro-tree?" Todd asked. "You're always really interested in environmental causes."

"I just have to make a real effort to present both sides as fairly as possible," Elizabeth said, hopping off the wall. "And to do that, I need to get quotes from both sides. Actually, I should start with you. Which side are you on?"

"I'm not sure," Todd answered. "I have friends on both sides. I want to be a loyal friend, but there's no way to do that without making some-body mad."

"But that's not how you should make up your mind," Elizabeth pointed out. "You don't have to support or fight a cause just because your friends are fighting or supporting it."

"Then how are we supposed to make up our minds?" Todd asked.

"By listening to both sides and seeing which one makes the most sense," Elizabeth answered. "And that's where I come in."

Jessica hurried into the empty art room and re-placed her sign. Her hands were shaking. She couldn't believe she had actually spoken to Mr. Clark like that. It made her feel sick and kind of ashamed. Maybe she was getting a little too carried away.

"Jessica?"

Jessica whirled to face the door and saw Aaron standing there with his hands in his pockets. "Hi," he said quietly.

"Hi," Jessica answered.

Aaron cleared his throat. "We haven't . . . uh . . . had too much time to talk in the last couple of days. But I know I sort of acted like a jerk about Lila and the soccer field."

"You sure did," Jessica agreed promptly.

"You don't have to agree so fast," Aaron shot back. "I mean, think about it from my position.

Here I am, the only sixth-grader on the team. Then suddenly there is no team. And then, thanks to Lila, there is. Wouldn't you be grateful?" He gave Jessica a sheepish smile. "I guess I was just so happy to be going to Division A, I couldn't help myself."

Jessica felt her lips beginning to curve into an involuntary smile. She'd forgotten how cute Aaron was. And how sweet he could be.

"At any rate," Aaron said, stepping a little closer, "I was wondering if . . . well . . . if I apologized, would you call off this SAVE THE TREES thing?"

Immediately the smile left Jessica's lips. She felt her face flush angrily. "No, I wouldn't!" she shouted.

Instantly Aaron's smile disappeared, and his face turned as angry as her own. "Look, Jessica!" he yelled. "Just because you're mad at me or mad at Lila, you don't have to punish the whole team and the whole school!"

"I'm not doing this because I'm mad at you!" Jessica shouted. "Why is that so hard for you to understand? I'm doing it because *I want to save the trees!*"

Jessica stalked past Aaron with her head held high. She didn't have any regrets or second thoughts now. She wasn't getting too carried away. There was no such thing as too carried away when you were fighting for something you believed in.

*   *   *

"Hey, Randy," Elizabeth called out, spotting him in the hall after first period. "I'm writing an article on the tree/soccer-field debate. May I ask you a couple of questions?"

"Sure," Randy responded.

Elizabeth opened her notebook and grabbed a pencil from her backpack. "OK," she said. "You were one of the leading fund-raisers for the soccer field. What made you change your mind about wanting to build it?"

Randy cleared his throat and pushed his glasses up on his nose. "When I found out the trees were four hundred years old, it made me realize that there are more important things in life than a soccer field."

"But you worked so hard to raise the money. Won't you feel some regret if the soccer field isn't built?"

Randy shook his head. "No. I don't think so. I think I'd rather keep the trees. They were here long before we came along, and I hope they'll be here long after we're gone."

"But why do you think the trees are so important?"

"They provide shade for people, homes for animals, and they're beautiful. The fight for them is symbolic of how important it is to protect our environment. After all, how can we ask the inhabitants of the Amazon rain forest not to cut down their trees if we're cutting down ours?"

"Thanks, Randy," Elizabeth said, making sure to get down everything exactly as he had said it.

"You're not going to call me a 'tree hugger' in your article, are you?" he asked uneasily.

"Of course not," Elizabeth replied. "My article is going to be objective."

Randy lifted an eyebrow. "Really? I was sort of hoping that you'd want to support us."

"I can't support either side," Elizabeth said, thinking back once again to her discussion with Mr. Bowman. "I'm a journalist. I have to be objective."

Randy frowned. "It seems as if the paper would have a duty to support us."

"A newspaper's duty is to present both sides fairly," Elizabeth said. Suddenly she caught sight of Rick Hunter. "Speaking of which, I need to get a quote from a member of the soccer-field faction. Thanks again, Randy," she said, hurrying after Rick.

"Rick!" she said when she caught up with him. "Can I get your thoughts on the soccer-field debate for *The Sixers*?"

"Sure," Rick answered with an easy smile. "I'm supporting the soccer field."

Rick Hunter was a nice-looking seventh-grader who usually got along well with everybody. Everybody except Jessica, that is. He loved to tease Jessica and make her mad, which was partially because he had a crush on her. So it didn't surprise Elizabeth that Jessica and Rick were on opposite sides.

"Why is that?" Elizabeth asked.

"The soccer field will give people more entertainment and exercise than the trees. After all, no one is talking about cutting them *all* down. But we can afford to sacrifice a *few* trees for the good of the whole school."

"But the trees are four hundred years old," Elizabeth said. "Yeah. And that seems really old to us. But that's only if we measure time by our own lifespans. The world is millions of years old. When you look at it that way, four hundred years isn't old—it's young."

"Thanks, Rick," Elizabeth said, taking down all his comments. "That's a good point."

She was really surprised at the thoughtful answers she was getting. Some people might be calling names and pointing fingers, but lots of people were really thinking.

"So will the paper be supporting the pro-soccer side?" he asked.

"The paper is going to present both sides fairly," Elizabeth answered firmly.

"Too bad," Rick said with a shrug. "Well, good luck."

"I think the paper should take a stand," Charlie Cashman said angrily. He had been standing a few feet away, listening to Elizabeth's conversation with Rick. "Objectivity is for cowards," he insisted. "You should tell the dumb tree huggers to get lost."

"Oh, yeah?" Winston Egbert growled, stepping

toward Charlie from the lockers that lined the opposite wall of the hallway. "Yeah!" Charlie said, taking a menacing step in Winston's direction.

"Hold it," Elizabeth said quickly. "It's not worth getting into a fight over."

Just then Ms. Wyler, their math teacher, stepped outside of her classroom and clapped her hands. "You two boys get to your classrooms right now," she ordered. "I don't care what you're arguing about. This school is not a boxing ring."

Charlie and Winston eyed each other angrily, but they obeyed, reluctantly backing away from each other and heading in two different directions.

Elizabeth sighed and scratched her head. Was she the only person in the whole school determined to remain objective and listen to both sides? Was that even the right approach to maintain? Maybe *The Sixers* should take a stand. But if it did, what stand should it take?

Elizabeth looked up at Ms. Wyler. Maybe the teachers could provide a consensus of reasonable opinion. They were grown-ups. They knew how to think things through and not get into silly squabbles.

"Ms. Wyler," Elizabeth said, "would you please give me a quote for *The Sixers* on your opinion of the pro-soccer versus the pro-tree dispute?"

"I'm a member of several nature clubs," Ms. Wyler answered thoughtfully, "and right or wrong, my tendency is to side with the pro-nature side of an argument."

"Thank you," Elizabeth said, scribbling quickly so that she could get Ms. Wyler's quote down word for word. But when she read it over and thought about it, she realized that Ms. Wyler's way of forming an opinion was just like Todd's. She wasn't thinking about the question—she was just siding with her friends.

"Mr. Clark," Elizabeth said, tapping softly at the door of his office.

Mr. Clark looked up from his work with a stern expression on his face. "Yes, Elizabeth?"

"Can I get a quote from you on the soccer-field situation?"

His face darkened. "There is no soccer-field situation," he answered curtly. "We have the money, the plans, and the go-ahead from the school board. The soccer-field construction will proceed as planned."

"But what about the trees?"

"There are plenty of trees," Mr. Clark said briskly. "But as we learned, not nearly enough soccer fields. And it doesn't make sense to get overly sentimental about something just because it's old."

"But . . ."

Mr. Clark pointed to the work on his desk. "I'm very busy right now, Elizabeth."

"Yes, sir," she said quietly, backing out the door.

Elizabeth stood in the hallway, taking notes for a few moments. Mr. Clark sounded just like Rick.

And Ms. Wyler sounded just like Todd. The grown-ups weren't turning out to be much help.

Then she thought about Mr. Sweeney, the art teacher. He was always talking about the importance of individualism and thinking for oneself. Maybe he would have something insightful to say.

He was alone in his classroom sketching at his desk when Elizabeth knocked softly on the open door on her way to lunch. Mr. Sweeney looked up and gave her a smile. "Hello, Elizabeth. What can I do for you?"

"I was wondering if you could give me your thoughts on the soccer-field controversy," she answered. "For *The Sixers*."

Mr. Sweeney sighed and put down his pencil. "Oh, boy! That's a toughie, isn't it?"

Elizabeth smiled. "I was hoping you had it figured out."

"Nobody has it figured out," Mr. Sweeney said with a smile. "Everyone wants to preserve our natural resources and protect our ecosystem," he said. "Including me."

"So you're on the pro-tree side?" she said.

"Not so fast," he said, lifting his palm. "That doesn't mean I think every single tree is irreplaceable. Or that trees are the most important thing around."

"I don't understand what you're saying," Elizabeth said with a puzzled frown.

"People are part of the ecosystem too," Mr. Sweeney said. "Recreation and athletic competition are legitimate human needs. Soccer is fun and it presents no threat to the environment. So I think that really, this argument is about conflicting values."

"But whose values are right?" Elizabeth persisted.

Mr. Sweeney smiled. "There's no answer to that question. It's a matter of preference. Some people would rather have trees. Some people would rather have a soccer field."

Elizabeth sighed. Everything Mr. Sweeney said made sense. But it was just a complicated way of saying, "I don't know."

"What's the matter?" Mr. Sweeney asked. "You look confused."

"I am confused," Elizabeth admitted. "Confused about how I feel about the issue. But I'm not confused anymore about whether or not the paper should take a stand. There are two sides to this story, and I have a duty to present them both."

"That's going to make some people unhappy," Mr. Sweeney warned.

"It already has," Elizabeth said with a sigh. "Thanks, Mr. Sweeney."

Ten

"Come sit here, Elizabeth!" Amy called.

Elizabeth realized as she walked into the crowded, noisy cafeteria that the room seemed to have split up into two camps: the pro-soccer-field side and the pro-tree side. And politics sure had formed some strange friendships.

The Unicorner was full of non-Unicorns. Grace Oliver seemed to have split off from the pro-soccer side and joined the pro-tree side of the cafeteria.

Jessica sat at a long table with Amy, Maria, Mandy, Grace, Lloyd, Sophia, Anna Reynolds, and Randy. Since Jessica, Mandy, and Grace were Unicorns, they normally wouldn't be caught dead sitting with Randy or Lloyd. But they were all talking excitedly. The tree issue seemed to have brought them all together.

Elizabeth sat down at Jessica's table, next to Amy.

"Hi," Maria said with a smile. "You must be having a field day. This thing is turning into a real media event."

"I'm glad you're here," Jessica said, eagerly pawing through her backpack. "Look." She handed Elizabeth several sheets of paper held together with a staple.

"What's this?" Elizabeth asked.

"Front-page news," Sarah said.

"It looks like a list of names," Elizabeth commented.

"Signatures," Amy corrected. "It's a petition demanding that the school cancel the construction of the soccer field."

Elizabeth smiled. "You should give this to Mr. Clark," she said. "Not me."

"But if we printed it in the paper, it would show the rest of the school how many people object to cutting down the trees," Amy argued. "We really should print it."

Jessica banged her fist down on the table. "You *have* to print it," she said in an angry voice. "Honestly, Elizabeth. I could understand your wanting to be objective when you thought it was just me and a few people who cared. But this petition proves that *everybody* cares. You might be the editor of the newspaper, but it's not *your* paper. It's everybody's paper. And it should take the side of the majority."

"But there's lots of support for the other side, too," Elizabeth argued reasonably.

"But the other side is wrong," Jessica cried.

"The other side has a different opinion," Elizabeth corrected.

"Why are you taking their side?" Amy demanded.

"I'm not taking anybody's side," Elizabeth replied, feeling stung. "You work on the paper too, Amy. You should know how important it is to tell both sides of the story."

"I don't think a newspaper should be afraid to distinguish between right and wrong," Amy said in a dark voice. "And actually, Elizabeth, I'm kind of disappointed in you."

"For trying to see both sides?" Elizabeth protested. "Well, I'm disappointed in you if you can't understand that I'm only trying to be fair!"

She looked around. All their faces had lost their friendly expressions.

Even Maria's face looked carefully blank. "I always thought of you as a sensitive person," she said softly.

"Maybe I'd better sit someplace else," Elizabeth said.

Nobody argued with her. Amy and Maria both looked down.

Elizabeth sighed and stood up, lifting her tray. "I'll see you guys later."

She looked around the cafeteria for someplace

else to sit. Then she realized she had lost her appetite. She dumped the contents of her tray into the garbage and started out of the cafeteria. She'd spend the rest of her lunch period in the library, working on her article.

On her way out, Aaron stopped her. "Elizabeth, I want to show you something."

"Sure, Aaron," she said a little warily.

He showed her several sheets of paper. "It's a petition. These are all the people who want the soccer field. I think *The Sixers* should print this on the front page."

"The other side has a petition too."

"Well, which side are you going to believe?" he asked.

"I believe that both sides feel very strongly about what they're doing."

Aaron angrily stuffed the petition into his book bag. "So you're against us."

"I didn't say I was against you."

"If you're not for us, you're against us," he said. "It's that simple."

Aaron stomped away. Elizabeth shook her head despondently. There was nothing simple about this at all.

"What can I do for you, Elizabeth?" Mr. Bowman asked when Elizabeth appeared in his doorway.

"*The Sixers* is due to be published tomorrow afternoon," Elizabeth answered with a heavy sigh. "And I just don't know what to do."

Mr. Bowman pointed to the empty chair by his desk. "Sit down," he said. "Are you having trouble sticking to the facts?" he asked.

Elizabeth reached into her backpack and removed the first draft of her story. "The problem is that there aren't a lot of facts. Just a lot of opinions. I've been really careful to present a balanced story. And I've quoted everybody word for word. But it still doesn't feel honest and objective. It's funny, Mr. Bowman, but it's as if everything is there but the truth. Some important part of the story is missing, and I don't know what it is."

Mr. Bowman leaned back in his chair. "You know," he said, "I was a reporter before I became a teacher. It was in the early seventies, when many people had very passionate opinions, especially about the Vietnam war. This really isn't a story about trees or soccer fields. It's a story about intensity of feeling. And that's what's missing from your story. Intensity of feeling. Passion. The passion on both sides."

"But you told me that I had to be objective," Elizabeth reminded him. "Remember the disaster with Mrs. Simmons and the Sweets for the Sweet Shop?"

"Of course. But I said that *you* had to be objective. That doesn't mean you can't print editorials.

An editorial is an opinion. And it's written by somebody who makes it very clear that they are not objective and aren't even trying to be."

Elizabeth sat up straighter. "Of course," she said happily. "Editorials from both sides! I'll ask for one from Jessica and one from Aaron. That should make everybody happy."

Mr. Bowman threw back his head and laughed. "I wouldn't count on it."

"I still don't see what the point of my writing an editorial was, if you were going to print one by Aaron, too," Jessica said angrily. "You even printed them on the same page. Side by side."

"Well, of course," Elizabeth answered impatiently. "The point was to make sure both of you had your say."

"But they just cancel each other out," Jessica complained. "So what's the point?"

"The point is that both sides of the argument are presented as fairly as possible," Elizabeth retorted. "And to tell you the truth, I'm sick of hearing people complain."

It was Thursday after school, and Elizabeth and Todd were sitting in Casey's, eating ice-cream sundaes. *The Sixers* had come out that morning. As promised, Elizabeth had done a straightforward job of reporting the events, and had presented everybody's side as fairly as she could. She had printed an editorial by Jessica and an editorial by Aaron.

As Mr. Bowman had predicted, nobody was happy.

"Traitor," she heard somebody hiss at her.

Elizabeth turned, glancing around Casey's, trying to figure out who was calling her names. Sadly, she realized it could have been anybody in the ice-cream parlor. Everybody there was a strong supporter of one side or the other of the debate.

Jessica stood up and threw down *The Sixers*. "I'm sick of people who won't stand up for what's right," she said angrily. "I'm going back to my picket line."

"Being objective is tough." Elizabeth sighed as she watched Jessica stomp away. "After all that work, not one single person has told me they liked the *Sixers* coverage of the story. Tons of people have told me they *didn't* like it. The only people who had anything good to say to me were Dennis Cookman and Alex Betner—and that's because I retracted what I said about them in the last issue."

"People are always talking about having the courage to take a stand," Todd said. "But it looks as if maybe it takes more courage *not* to take a stand."

Elizabeth stirred her ice cream until it was nice and soupy. Outside the window she saw Jessica, Amy, Maria, and Winston marching back and forth in front of the ice-cream parlor, waving their SAVE THE TREES signs.

Bruce Patman, Peter Jefferies, and Denny Jacobson were sitting in the booth by the window.

Bruce rapped his knuckles against the glass. "Tree huggers!" he shouted. "You'll look pretty stupid tomorrow, crying over trees that aren't there anymore!"

Immediately Amy and Maria stuck out their tongues at Bruce, and Jessica and Winston came running to the door. "You'll look pretty stupid tomorrow yourself!" Jessica shouted in the doorway.

"Oh, yeah? The bulldozer is due at ten A.M. tomorrow," Bruce countered.

Jessica gave him a smirk. "We'll just see about that. We've got a plan to stop the construction, and there's nothing you can do about it."

Elizabeth's heart sank. Jessica's plans almost always meant trouble for somebody. Most of the time, it meant trouble for Jessica.

Winston and Jessica began parading through Casey's, waving their signs in the air. "Save the trees! Save the trees! Save the trees!" they chanted.

"Save the trees! Save the trees!" people all around began to shout.

"Save the soccer field!" Bruce and Rick shouted. "Save the soccer field!"

Cries of "Save the soccer field!" began to be heard all through the ice-cream parlor.

Elizabeth shook her head. "There must be some better way for people to resolve their differences."

"Yeah! People should be able to compromise," Todd said.

"But you heard Jessica," Elizabeth said. " 'Two,

four, six, eight. We will not negotiate.' I know how Jessica is when she's got her teeth in something. You just can't reason with her."

Bruce and his buddies were now standing on the chairs, making rude noises and laughing at the demonstrators.

"I get the feeling they're *enjoying* themselves," Todd said mournfully.

"Jessica's not enjoying herself," Elizabeth replied quickly.

"No?"

As Elizabeth watched, Jessica climbed up on a chair and began to wave her fist high in the air. "Nature lovers, unite!" she yelled. "Save the trees!"

"Well," Elizabeth admitted, "maybe she is—just a little."

"Uh-oh," Todd said. "Here comes Mr. Casey. And he doesn't look like *he's* enjoying this at all."

Mr. Casey came hurrying out of the back of the ice-cream parlor. He looked furious. "Stop this right now!" he bellowed. "*Get down off of that chair and leave this establishment immediately!*" he shouted at Bruce.

"BOOOOO!" some of the kids began to yell.

Mr. Casey glared at Jessica. "*You and your friends get out too.*"

"Save the trees!" Jessica shouted defiantly.

Mr. Casey took a deep breath, and as Elizabeth watched in awe, he seemed to explode. "*I said, OUT!*" he yelled in a voice that split the air like a foghorn.

Immediately the kids were silent.

"I'll give you ten seconds to clear out of here," Mr. Casey said ominously.

Both factions scrambled for the door, and within seconds, the ice-cream parlor was silent.

"Ahhhh," Todd said. "Finally! I can hear myself think."

Mr. Casey turned toward Todd. "Hey!" he barked at Todd and Elizabeth. "I told you kids to clear out. Come back when you're through making trouble."

"But we weren't making any trouble," Todd protested. "We're not—we don't—I haven't even finished my ice cream."

"I don't care," Mr. Casey said. "OUT!"

Elizabeth quickly grabbed her backpack and Todd's arm as Mr. Casey hustled them out.

"That does it!" Todd shouted angrily as the door slammed behind them. "I'm through with being neutral. It's impossible."

"You are?" Elizabeth gasped. "Which side are you going to support?"

"Neither!" Todd said, hoisting his backpack onto his shoulder. "I'm against *both*!"

Eleven

"*Save the trees!*" Jessica shouted, waving her sign.

"*Save the trees!*" she heard her followers shout.

After leaving Casey's, the pro-tree faction had decided to march back to school and demonstrate outside for a while.

"You know, Jessica," Winston said, coming up to walk beside her, "I always thought you were . . . I don't know . . . sort of silly. But I really admire the way you've gotten everybody united behind this cause."

Amy came over and patted her on the shoulder. "Winston's right. You're turning out to be a really strong leader. And we're going to need a strong leader to pull off our plan tomorrow. It's a brilliant idea, Jess. How did you think of it?"

"I didn't," Jessica said. "I saw some people do it

on the news once." Thinking about the following day produced a little flicker of fear in her stomach. The plan was so audacious and daring, she could hardly even believe she'd gotten so many people to agree to it. Maybe it was a little *too* audacious and daring. "You don't think we're going overboard, do you?" she asked Amy.

"Are you kidding? There's no such thing as going overboard when you're saving trees that are four hundred years old."

"What do you think, Winston?"

"I'm with Amy," he answered firmly. "And with you."

"They're all with you," Amy said, gesturing to the growing crowd behind Jessica.

Jessica grinned and held her head up high. She'd never felt so good about herself in her whole life. Lois Lattimer was right. Activism was fun.

"Dad?" Elizabeth said when she got home that afternoon.

Mr. Wakefield put the newspaper down and smiled. "What can I do for the star reporter in the family?"

"I need some advice," Elizabeth said, plopping down on the sofa.

"That's what I'm here for. Even though it is supposed to be my afternoon off," he added with a little laugh. "Let me see if I can guess what you need advice about—Jessica and the trees?"

Elizabeth nodded. "You're a lawyer. You have to settle all kinds of arguments. What do you do when people on different sides of an argument refuse to compromise?"

Mr. Wakefield sighed. "Well, first of all, you're a reporter, not a lawyer. I'm not sure it's your job to negotiate a settlement. Your job is to stay neutral, print the truth as best you can, and report the facts."

"That's what Mr. Bowman says," Elizabeth murmured. "But I'm also a student at Sweet Valley Middle School. And this is tearing our school apart. There must be some way I can help to solve this without . . ." she hesitated, trying to figure out how to say it.

"Compromising your neutrality?" Mr. Wakefield finished for her.

"Exactly," Elizabeth said. It was amazing how quickly her father was able to find the right words sometimes.

"Well," Mr. Wakefield said thoughtfully, "sometimes an inability to compromise is based on too much emotion and not enough information."

"What do you mean?"

"When I have a case where the sides refuse to compromise, I try to find out everything I can about the subject of the dispute. Sometimes I'll unearth some piece of information that makes one side of the argument or the other emerge as the most convincing."

Elizabeth stood up.

"Where are you going?" Mr. Wakefield asked.

"To the Nature Society," Elizabeth answered. "I think it's time for a little investigative reporting."

"Hi," Bill Watkins said, smiling warmly at Elizabeth. "Where's your sister today?"

"Leading a protest march around the school," Elizabeth answered.

"Really?" Bill asked with a laugh. "I guess she decided to get serious about those trees."

"She sure did," Elizabeth agreed. "But lots of kids are serious about wanting a soccer field, too. Even the teachers and parents are getting involved in the argument. It's split the whole school in half."

"That's too bad," Bill said. "Causes should bring people together, not tear them apart."

"Not if everybody supports different causes," Elizabeth said. "How can you get people to agree?"

"If I knew that, I'd be president, or king, or leader of the world," Bill replied.

Elizabeth sighed heavily. "I was hoping you could help me find the answer."

"Sometimes there isn't an answer," Bill said. "But there's always a solution."

"That's sort of what my dad said. He said I might find the solution if I start looking for more information."

"That's true. And if you want information, you've come to the right place. We've got a whole library full of books. What kind of information are you looking for?"

"I'm not sure. But I guess I should start by finding out more about the trees. We don't even know what kind they are. I looked through the pamphlets you gave us, but I didn't see any trees that looked exactly like our trees."

"Then come this way," Bill said, leading her toward a room off the main lobby.

Inside, there were shelves and shelves of books. "What are all these books about?" Elizabeth asked.

"Everything under the sun, everything over the sun, and the sun," Bill replied with a laugh. "We buy every book we can afford to purchase on nature, the environment, and space. Anything that relates to the planet."

He went over to one of the shelves and began pulling books out. "I'm going to give you some books on trees that are indigenous to this area of California," he said. "They have lots of pictures, so you should be able to identify the trees you're worried about."

Bill took the books over to a desk and made a note of their titles. Then he pushed the little piece of paper toward Elizabeth. "Just write down your name, address, and phone number. Then you're welcome to take them home. You can keep them for three weeks."

"Thanks," Elizabeth said. "But I don't have three weeks. I only have until tomorrow at ten A.M."

*   *   *

Late that night there was a soft knock at Elizabeth's bedroom door.

"Come in," she said.

The door opened, and Mr. Wakefield stuck his head in. "I saw the light on under your door. It's almost midnight. What are you doing up so late?"

Elizabeth turned the page of the big book she was reading. "Trying to get more information," she replied.

"Well, don't stay up too much longer," he warned. "It'll be morning earlier than you think."

"I won't," Elizabeth promised as he shut the door. She yawned and rubbed her eyes. She'd been looking through the books for hours now, and her eyelids were feeling heavy. So far she hadn't found any information that would change somebody's mind. But just then, as she turned the page, something caught her eye and she sat up a little straighter.

It was a picture of a tree. A tree just like the ones that stood behind the school. And something about the picture looked very familiar.

In the photograph there was a big circle around the bark at the base of the tree. Elizabeth quickly removed her magnifying glass from her desk drawer and examined the picture more closely. "Ah ha," she breathed. "I think I'm finally onto something."

Twelve

The leaves underneath Elizabeth's feet crackled as she walked quickly through the woods early the next morning.

The book on trees she'd been reading was tucked under her arm, and a magnifying glass was stuck in her back pocket.

She walked up to one of the trunks and examined it closely. Then she opened up her book and looked at the picture. It showed a section of bark that looked patchy and yellowish.

Again Elizabeth looked at the trunk of the tree. There were several sections where the bark looked patchy and yellowish. She pressed her finger against the patch. It was spongy and soft, not hard like the rest of the trunk.

Elizabeth took her magnifying glass from her

back pocket and examined the patch. Through the glass, the bark of the tree looked even more like the picture in the book.

She moved over to the next tree. The trunk of that tree had yellowish spongy patches on it too.

So did the next tree. And the next. And the one next to that.

Every tree that Elizabeth examined had the same yellowish spongy patches on it.

Elizabeth sucked in her breath. She was pretty sure she had just discovered something important. Something that would probably put the whole pro-tree/pro-soccer debate to rest.

"Elizabeth! What are you doing here?" Jessica demanded, suddenly appearing from behind a large tree trunk.

"Jessica," Elizabeth said eagerly. "I'm so glad you're here. Look! I have some information you should know about." Elizabeth held the book out toward Jessica, but Jessica took a step back.

"I have all the information I need," Jessica said. "What I want to know is what you're doing here. Are you trying to spy for the other side?"

"Of course not," Elizabeth said angrily. "I'm trying to keep things from getting out of hand. Listen, Jess, I know you've got some kind of plan up your sleeve," she continued, trying to keep her voice calm. "But I think you should look at this book before you do anything silly."

"So it's silly to try to save trees?" Jessica cried.

"Stop twisting my words around, and look at this book!" Elizabeth said, suddenly losing her temper. "I know you feel really passionate about this, but that doesn't mean you can't be reasonable, too."

"Why should I listen to you?" Jessica demanded. "You don't care about trees, and you don't care about me. If you did, you would be on my side."

"Jessica!" Elizabeth pleaded. "Please listen."

But before she could say another word, the school bell rang.

"Sorry, Elizabeth," Jessica said, tossing her hair defiantly off of her shoulders. "It's time for action."

And with that, Jessica turned and ran toward the school.

"Wait, Jessica!" Elizabeth shouted, running after her. "What are you going to do?"

"Wait and see," Jessica called over her shoulder.

Elizabeth jogged to a stop. Jessica was going to do something stupid, she just knew it. And she was going to do it for no reason at all.

The bell rang again, signaling that homeroom was about to start.

Suddenly Elizabeth had an idea. The secretary in Mr. Clark's office would probably let her use the phone, she thought as she started running toward the school. It was early, but she just had to hope it wasn't too early to reach Bill Watkins at the Nature Society.

*   *   *

Jessica sat in her second-period class, chewing nervously on her nail. She reached under her desk and felt for her backpack, assuring herself that it was within easy reach.

Ms. Wyler's voice droned on and on, but Jessica could hardly pay attention. Her heart was racing so fast, and beating so hard, it was making a drumming sound in her ears.

She glanced at Amy Sutton, and saw that Amy was darting nervous glances back in her direction. Jessica forced herself to smile reassuringly. The pro-tree group was nervous. But Jessica was their leader, and it was her job to give them courage. She tried hard to look brave. But inside she felt far from brave. She felt scared. Still, she had never felt so exhilarated in her life. She was doing something important. Something that counted. Something that was going to benefit people other than herself.

Far in the distance, she thought she heard a rumbling sound.

She cut her eyes back in Amy's direction. Amy's head was cocked, and she was frowning, as if she was straining to hear.

Jessica closed her eyes and listened hard. The rumbling sound was getting louder. She turned in her seat and saw Winston Egbert giving her a wide-eyed, nervous look. Behind Winston, Jessica saw Maria Slater shift slightly in her seat and reach down for her own backpack.

Suddenly the rumbling sound became louder, as if some large and heavy piece of machinery was approaching the school.

There was the grinding sound of an engine, and then the loud, unmistakable sound of a bulldozer.

"It's zero hour!" Jessica shouted, jumping up from her seat and grabbing her backpack.

Before the words were out of her mouth, Amy, Winston, and Maria jumped up too.

"Let's move!" Jessica shouted, running for the door.

"Sit down!" Ms. Wyler ordered in a loud voice. "Return to your seats immediately!"

But Jessica and her followers didn't pay a bit of attention. Instead, they ran into the halls.

"It's zero hour!" Maria shouted, running the length of the hall.

Kids began pouring out of classrooms, all of them carrying their backpacks.

Jessica and Amy ran past the rest rooms.

"Zero hour!" Jessica shouted, banging her fist on the door of the girls' bathroom.

"Zero hour!" Amy shouted, banging her fist on the door of the boys' bathroom.

The doors opened. Randy Mason came running out of the boys' bathroom, and Mandy Miller came running out of the girls' bathroom.

Jessica pushed the side door of the school open and dashed outside. She saw a bulldozer lumbering slowly toward the trees. She cast a look behind her, and her heart soared when she saw the huge crowd of kids that was running behind her. They were following her. Her! Jessica Wakefield! Their leader!

"Come back inside!" she heard Mr. Clark's voice bellow over the noise of the bulldozer. *"Come back inside right now!"*

Jessica looked behind her again and saw Mr. Clark, Mrs. Knight, Mr. Sweeney, and several other teachers chasing the students.

More and more kids were pouring out of the school now. The pro-soccer faction was chasing the teachers. Lila, Janet, Peter, Aaron, Bruce, Denny, and dozens of other kids were streaming out of the doors.

Jessica raced past the bulldozer and saw the driver do a double take when he saw her and all the other kids running behind her.

She ran over to a tree, reached into her backpack, and removed a bicycle chain and padlock.

SNAP! went the lock as Jessica chained herself to the trunk of the tree, wrapping the chain around her waist and the thick trunk. "Now try to bulldoze this tree!" she yelled at the driver.

SNAP! SNAP!

Amy and Maria chained themselves to the trees next to Jessica.

SNAP! SNAP!

Winston and Randy chained themselves to two other trees.

SNAP! SNAP! SNAP!

Kids were chaining themselves to trees all over the woods.

The bulldozer idled in neutral with its engine grinding loudly, and the driver jumped out. "Mr. Clark," the driver shouted. "Would you please do something about this? I don't have all day."

"Expel them, Mr. Clark!" Bruce Patman yelled.

"Throw them out of school!" Charlie Cashman demanded. "We can't let them push the rest of us around!"

"*Tree huggers!*" Bruce Patman began to chant. "*Tree huggers!*"

"Stop this immediately, or I will suspend every one of you!" Mr. Clark shouted.

"We refuse to leave until you agree to cancel the soccer field," Jessica shouted. "*Right?*"

All the pro-tree demonstrators raised their fists in the air. "*Right!*"

"*Tree huggers!*" the pro-soccer faction shouted.

"*Tree killers!*" the pro-tree faction shouted.

"STOP THIS RIGHT NOW!" Mr. Clark bellowed.

"Do something about these kids!" the bulldozer driver demanded.

"Hold it!" cried another voice.

Jessica lifted her hand for silence as Elizabeth came running toward the group, followed by Bill Watkins from the Nature Society.

She's changed her mind, Jessica thought happily.

She's decided to be on my side after all. And she's brought Bill to convince everybody how important the trees are.

Jessica had never felt so proud and happy in her whole life. That's probably what Elizabeth had been trying to tell her this morning—that she'd been wrong, and Jessica had been right.

She watched as Bill ran up to Mr. Clark and the two of them talked quietly for a moment. Mr. Clark frowned and nodded his head, looking very interested in what Bill was telling him.

So Mr. Clark was changing his mind too.

They would all change their minds. The trees would be saved. And it would all be due to Jessica's efforts as an activist.

She swallowed the lump that was rising in her throat and blinked back happy tears when Mr. Clark waved his hand to the bulldozer driver, signaling him to turn off his engine.

The driver rolled his eyes and turned off the engine.

Immediately the noise level was reduced.

"Hooray!" shouted the pro-tree faction.

Mr. Clark held up his hands for silence. "May I have your attention, please? This is Bill Watkins, a scientist from the Nature Society. He wants to examine our trees."

"Examine our trees?" Winston asked.

Students on both sides began to whisper among themselves as Bill stepped over to one of the trees and pulled out his pocketknife. He scraped at the bark of one of the trees, then stared down at the blade of the knife.

After a long moment, he sighed. "Yep! They're going to have to come down, all right!"

Thirteen

"What do you mean, they have to come down?" Jessica cried.

"Cut down the trees?" Mandy exclaimed.

"What kind of environmentalist are you?" Winston demanded.

Bill Watkins motioned to all the students to come in closer so that they could hear. "Listen to me, please." He scraped at the bark of one of the trees again with his knife. "Look at this," he said, holding the blade of the knife toward Jessica.

Jessica frowned down at the knife. "So?"

"Watch it carefully."

Elizabeth stepped over to Jessica and handed her the magnifying glass. "Here," she said. "Look through this."

Jessica peered at the knife blade through the

magnifying glass, and her eyes widened. "It's moving."

Bill nodded. "That's right." He held the knife out for Winston and Randy to see. "It's moving because it's full of tiny bugs. Bugs that move in when a tree is diseased and dying. Rotting away."

He wiped the blade on a rag and put the knife away. "If you look around, you'll see that all of these trees have yellowish patches on the bark. That means they're full of these bugs. These trees are actually a hazard. If they're not all cut down, the bugs can spread the disease and eventually kill a lot of the trees in Sweet Valley."

There was a moment of stunned silence.

"You mean all the trees have to go?" Aaron asked softly. "The entire woods? Not just the trees that are blocking the soccer field?"

"I'm afraid so," Bill said solemnly.

"We won't have any woods left at all," Aaron said slowly.

"Are the trees dying of old age?" Amy asked.

Bill shook his head. "Oh, no. These trees aren't that old. They just have a very common tree disease."

"But we thought the trees were four hundred years old," Winston said, darting a look at Jessica.

"What made you think that?" Bill asked.

"Jessica!" the entire pro-tree faction said at once.

"Bill, *you* said the trees around here were four hundred years old," Jessica said, her cheeks flushing red. "You told me and Elizabeth that the day we came to see you at the Nature Society."

"I said *some* of the trees in Sweet Valley were four hundred years old. But not these. These trees are probably around sixty years old." He smiled reassuringly. "Don't worry too much about these trees. They're not so old or rare. You see a lot of them around this part of California."

Suddenly Bruce burst into laughter. "You guys caused all this trouble over a bunch of ordinary trees that are full of bugs. What a bunch of idiots!"

All around Bruce there were snickers.

Amy turned to Jessica, her face pale and angry. "Gee, thanks, Jessica. You made fools out of us."

SNAP! Winston unchained himself and stuffed the chain into his backpack. "Didn't it even occur to you to find out a little bit more about this before you got us all involved?"

SNAP! Randy unchained himself too. "I feel really stupid."

Jessica unchained herself with shaking hands. She had never felt so completely and utterly humiliated in her life.

"I can't believe we worked so hard to save a few young, dying trees," Maria muttered darkly as she pushed angrily past Jessica.

"So what do you want to do about these trees?" the bulldozer driver asked. "My contract is only to clear a four-yard strip. If you want them all to come down, it's going to be a pretty big project. Expensive, too."

Mr. Clark ran his hand wearily through his hair. "You'd better meet me in my office and give me an estimate. I'll have to call an emergency meeting of the PTA and the school board tonight. Let's all get back to class now." He clapped his hands. "Come on. Come on," he barked at the students. "Go back inside. The excitement is over for today."

Jessica looked up and saw Lila and Janet pointing to her and whispering. Lila said something, and Janet began to giggle. Then they both whispered something to Aaron. Lila and Janet giggled again, but Aaron's face was solemn as he watched Jessica. Lila pulled at his sleeve, and then the three of them turned and walked back toward the school.

Halfway across the field, Aaron looked over his shoulder at Jessica. Then he shook his head and turned away again.

Jessica walked stiffly through the woods, still numb with shock. She just couldn't face going back to school yet.

"I'm sorry," she heard a soft voice say.

Jessica turned and saw Elizabeth step out from behind a clump of trees.

"Why didn't you tell me?" Jessica demanded. "Why did you let me make such a fool out of myself?"

"I tried," Elizabeth reminded her. "I tried this

morning, but you wouldn't listen."

Jessica hung her head miserably. "You did try to tell me," she said, her voice choking with tears. "Why didn't I listen?"

"Because you cared so much about what you were doing," Elizabeth said.

"I cared *too* much," Jessica said bitterly. "It's better not to care about things."

"That's not true," Elizabeth protested. "See? You're doing it again. Just going from one extreme to the other. It's important to care about things. But you have to try to be reasonable, too."

Jessica picked up her backpack.

"Are you coming back inside?" Elizabeth asked.

"No," Jessica said, trying to stifle a sob. "I'm going home. I can't face anyone at school."

"Jessica!"

But Jessica was already running deeper into the woods. Tears of embarrassment and anger were running down her cheeks. She'd made a fool of herself. She'd made fools out of her supporters. She'd alienated all the Unicorns. She didn't have a friend left in the world.

All around her there was a deep, still silence. Not one bird was cheeping or singing, and Jessica felt as though even they had decided not to speak to her.

Fourteen

"So don't forget, kids," Lois Lattimer was saying. "Activism is fun. So get out there and work for the environment. Save the . . ."

CLICK!

Jessica stared for a moment at the blank television screen. She didn't want to hear one more word about trees, activism, the environment, or anything else. It made her feel sick to think about it.

She looked at the clock. It was almost six o'clock. Her parents had left a message on the answering machine saying that they were going from work to the emergency PTA meeting at school. Elizabeth had called and left a message that she was going to go to the meeting to cover it for *The Sixers*.

The front door opened, and Jessica's heart began to thump. Were they home already? She knew she was going to be in big trouble once her parents found out everything that had happened that morning.

But it wasn't her parents. It was Steven.

"Well, look who's here," he teased. "Sweet Valley's very own Lois Lattimer."

"Shut up," Jessica muttered.

Steven plopped down on the sofa and began to laugh. "A bunch of people at high school have been talking about you."

Jessica felt her ears turning red. She could just see all the high-school kids laughing at her and saying what a pinhead she was. She flopped facedown on the sofa and groaned into the cushions.

"What are you groaning about?" Steven asked. "You're always saying how you want to be famous. Now you are."

"Famous for being an idiot," she groaned.

"You'll live it down," he assured her.

"No, I won't," she said. "Nobody at school is speaking to me. I'm going to get grounded for skipping school this afternoon. My life is ruined."

Steven let out a little laugh. "Don't get so carried away. Your demonstration backfired. But look at it this way. If it hadn't been for all the trouble you caused, they might not have discovered the tree disease, and we might have lost a lot of the trees in Sweet Valley."

Jessica raised her head a little so she could see

Steven's face. Was he serious, or was he just pulling her leg?

He tossed a pillow at her. "You did something good, Jessica. Though it may take a while for people to see that, after what a pain in the neck you've been. And you sure have been a pain in the neck."

"Ohhh," Jessica groaned, burying her face in a pillow. "I wish I were dead."

Steven laughed. "You probably will be, once Mom and Dad get home."

Just then the front door opened and Mr. and Mrs. Wakefield walked in, with Elizabeth close behind. All three looked depressed and tired.

Jessica shrank a little when she saw her parents' faces.

"We have a lot to talk about, young lady," her mother said in a stern voice.

"I know," Jessica squeaked. "I'm sorry."

"Sorry doesn't explain going off half-cocked, chaining yourself to a tree, disrupting morning classes, and then skipping school this afternoon," Mr. Wakefield said.

"I guess you talked to Mr. Clark," Jessica said miserably.

"Yes, we did."

"Yell at Jessica later," Steven suggested. "Tell me what happened at the meeting."

Mr. Wakefield sat down on the sofa. "It's going to be very expensive to clear all those woods," Mr. Wakefield said. "Far more expensive than we imagined." He shook his head sadly. "There won't be enough money left for the soccer field."

"That's terrible," Steven said. "So the middle school is going to lose their trees *and* the soccer field?"

Mr. Wakefield nodded. "I'm afraid so. The school board has no surplus in its budget. No one feels it's appropriate to ask Mr. Fowler to donate any more money. So it looks as though that's what we're stuck with for the present."

"Well," Jessica said, trying to make her voice sound casual. "If that's that, then I guess I'll go up to my room and—"

"And stay there," Mr. Wakefield finished sharply. "You're grounded, Jessica."

"Yes, sir," Jessica whispered.

I wonder if Lois Lattimer ever has days like this, she thought as she trudged heavily up the stairs.

"If it's any consolation," Elizabeth said glumly later that night, "I got in trouble too. Mr. Bowman yelled at me *again*. From now on he wants to discuss every story before it gets printed. He said this whole thing was almost as much my fault as it was yours." She cringed inside, remembering the stern lecture he had given her.

"Why does he think that?" Jessica asked.

Elizabeth settled down on Jessica's bed and put her chin in her hands.

"Because it was my job to check the facts. And if

I'd checked the facts about the trees before I started writing, none of this would have happened. I jumped to the same conclusions you did."

"Gee," Jessica said, brightening a bit. "I guess it *is* partially your fault."

"You don't have to be so happy about it," Elizabeth grumbled. "I'm in a lot of trouble. In fact, after the week I've had, I'm ready to hang up my pad and pencil for good."

"Oh, Lizzie, no you're not," Jessica said with a sigh. "Besides, I can't help it. I'm miserable, and misery loves company. And since nobody is speaking to me, and I'm grounded until Monday, you're the only company I've got."

"Nobody's speaking to me, either," Elizabeth said unhappily. "Everybody is really mad that the paper didn't take sides, or get the facts soon enough."

Jessica sighed. "I guess we both goofed up pretty big time."

Elizabeth sighed too. "As activists and journalists, we stink. Maybe we should start looking for different careers."

Jessica tossed and turned. Her mind kept replaying the awful events of that morning, and it made it impossible to go to sleep. She got out of bed, went over to the window, and sighed as she looked out.

Lots of people seemed to be up, because lots of lights were still on in the houses along the street. What were all those people doing awake? she wondered. Were they worrying too much to fall asleep too? Well, at least they wouldn't have to worry about sick trees anymore.

Jessica remembered what Steven had said. If it hadn't been for all the trouble she and Elizabeth caused, the tree disease wouldn't have been discovered, and then it would have spread and killed a lot of the trees in Sweet Valley.

She went back over to her bed. *I need to remember to tell Elizabeth that,* she thought as she pulled the covers up to her chin. *If she's going to share the blame, she might as well share some of the credit, too.* She flopped over onto her stomach. *Not that anybody's going to give us any.*

Jessica sat straight up in bed. She blinked at the bright sunlight streaming into her window. It was morning, and she'd just awakened with an incredibly brilliant, incredibly logical, incredibly incredible idea.

She threw back the covers and ran for the door. *"Elizabeth!"* she shouted.

Jessica thundered down the stairs and hurried into the kitchen.

Elizabeth, Steven, and Mr. and Mrs. Wakefield were already gathered at the breakfast table.

"I just woke up with a brilliant idea," Jessica announced as she entered the kitchen.

"Uh-oh," Steven said. "Jessica's getting ideas again. Look out."

"Steady, Jessica," Mr. Wakefield warned, looking up from his newspaper.

"Don't get carried away," Elizabeth begged.

"Look before you leap," Mrs. Wakefield cautioned.

"Listen!" Jessica exclaimed in an urgent voice. "Bill Watkins said that if the trees don't get cut down, the disease could spread and kill a lot of the trees in Sweet Valley, right?"

"Right . . ." Mr. Wakefield said.

"So it's in the best interests of the whole community to cut down the trees, right?"

"Right . . ." Mrs. Wakefield said.

"So shouldn't the whole community *share* in the cost of clearing the woods?"

Mr. Wakefield's eyes widened. Mrs. Wakefield sat up straighter. Elizabeth's mouth fell open.

"*Right!*" they all said at the same time.

"You really are thinking now," Mr. Wakefield said, jumping up from the breakfast table.

"Where are you going?" Jessica asked as she hurried after him into his study.

"I'm going to call Mr. Clark at home," he said, flipping through the phone book. "I think you may have just saved the soccer field *and* the trees."

Elizabeth and Jessica hurried into the assembly on Monday morning and sat down in the front row. Jessica couldn't help but notice the glances she was getting.

"Do you know what this assembly is about?" Jessica heard Amy ask Mary. The two girls were sitting in the row behind Jessica and Elizabeth.

"It's about the woods and the soccer field," Mary answered, casting a quick glance at Jessica.

"My mom went to the PTA meeting last Friday. It looks like we're going to lose out on both," Amy said.

"Maybe not," Jessica whispered to Elizabeth.

Elizabeth lifted her hand and showed Jessica that her fingers were crossed for luck.

Mr. Clark stepped up to the podium and rapped on it for attention. "Quiet, please!"

The students fell silent, and Mr. Clark cleared his throat. "As you all know," he began, "there has been a great deal of controversy surrounding the trees behind our school. As it turns out, the entire woods must be cleared in order to prevent the spread of a tree disease throughout our community."

There was an unhappy rustle through the auditorium.

"The cost of clearing those woods is much higher than we anticipated. As of Friday afternoon, it appeared that once the work was finished, there would not be sufficient money left over to enlarge our soccer field."

A few groans floated through the auditorium.

"But then I received a phone call from the parents of one of our students over the weekend. It seems that student had a very helpful idea. That student pointed out that the entire Sweet Valley Community had a vested interest in removing the diseased trees, and therefore had a responsibility to share in the cost of their removal."

There were excited whispers from the audience.

"I have just gotten off the phone with the City Council. They agreed with this student, and as a result, they have pledged to cover a sufficient percentage of the costs so that we now have enough money to complete the soccer field, and even a little left over. I think we should all have a round of applause for the student whose clear thinking provided us with this constructive solution to our problem—Jessica Wakefield."

The entire auditorium burst into enthusiastic applause.

"I'm really proud of you," Elizabeth whispered, giving Jessica a hug. "That was really good thinking."

"Thanks," Jessica said. "I'm kind of proud of me too."

It was great hearing the applause, but Jessica noticed that a lot of cold looks were still being directed at her. Soccer field or no soccer field, she knew that she had completely alienated an awful lot of people. They might be applauding her for coming up with a good idea, but that didn't mean they were going to forgive and forget. A lot of ugly things had been said over the last few days. And a lot of them had been said by Jessica.

"Let's be sure to go to the cafeteria together at lunch," she whispered to Elizabeth. "That way, if people still aren't speaking to us, we'll have somebody to sit with."

"Good thinking," Elizabeth whispered back.

"Where is everybody?" Jessica asked with a frown.

Elizabeth shook her head in confusion. "I don't know. This is really weird."

There were hardly any students in the cafeteria. And those who were there began to whisper and nudge each other when they saw Jessica and Elizabeth.

"I can't imagine where everybody is," Elizabeth exclaimed. "Was there an assembly or something that we didn't hear about?"

Jessica frowned. "I don't think so. Geez, Lizzie, I knew that a lot of people would probably avoid us at lunch, but I didn't know they would avoid the whole cafeteria."

"Shhh," Elizabeth said. "What's that noise?"

Jessica cocked her head and listened. "It's coming from outside, and it's getting louder."

"Let's go see what's going on," Elizabeth said, grabbing Jessica's hand.

The two girls hurried out into the hall and pushed open the side door.

"Save the trees! Save the trees!" roared a huge

mob of students who were gathered outside.

Jessica blinked. What was going on? It looked as though the whole school was gathered out there.

As she scanned the crowd in astonishment she saw Amy Sutton, Maria Slater, Winston Egbert, Peter Jefferies, Denny Jacobson, and Aaron Dallas all shouting and holding up signs that said SAVE THE TREES.

"I don't get it," Elizabeth said. "I thought the SAVE THE TREES campaign was over."

Amy smiled at Jessica and Elizabeth. She stepped forward out of the crowd and held up her hand for silence. "The SAVE THE TREES campaign is still on," she said.

"A lot of us have been talking since this morning's assembly," Aaron said, looking directly at Jessica and smiling. "Losing the woods has made all of us realize how much the trees mean to us."

"But the trees are diseased," Elizabeth said. "We can't save them."

"No," Aaron agreed. "But we can plant more trees in their place. The guy from the Nature Society said the trees were easily replaced. So we figured we'd all get on the same team this time around. We'll work together to plant new trees as soon as the new soccer field goes in."

"But new trees cost money," Jessica pointed out.

"That's right," Randy Mason said. "And the sooner we start the collection campaign, the sooner we can raise the money and start planting. Mr.

Clark has agreed to make the first contribution out of what's left in the soccer-field fund. But we're going to need someone to lead the drive." He looked around at all the faces in the crowd. "And we thought you would be the perfect person."

"Me?" Jessica cried.

"Sure," Randy said. "Look at how successful you were at raising money for the soccer field."

"And look at how successful you were at organizing the SAVE THE TREES campaign," Maria added.

"What do you say, Jessica?" Aaron asked softly.

Jessica's face broke into a broad grin. "I'll do it under one condition," she said, grabbing her sister's hand. "Only if we get full coverage from the world's greatest sixth-grade journalist."

"And that could only be Elizabeth Wakefield," Amy said, smiling at Elizabeth.

"What do *you* say, Elizabeth?" Jessica asked.

Elizabeth laughed. "I say . . . *Save the trees!*"

Fifteen

◇

"If I hear one more word about you getting a letter from Lois Lattimer, I'm going to throw up," Lila complained.

"You're just jealous," Jessica said happily, digging her shovel into the ground.

It was a sunny Tuesday afternoon two weeks later, and a big crowd of middle schoolers—from both the pro-tree and pro-soccer-field factions—was outside planting the first batch of tree saplings.

"I am not," Lila said, throwing her own shovel down. "I'm just tired of listening to you brag."

Elizabeth and Amy exchanged a grin as they dropped a sapling into the hole that Lila and Jessica had dug. Things were pretty much back to normal—except that now the school had a brand-new soccer field, the woods were gone, and Jessica had collected so much money at the mall that they'd already been able to buy almost as many trees as they'd lost.

"*I'm* tired of listening to you two argue," Amy said. "You've been at it all afternoon."

"I'm tired of arguing too," Lila said. "I just wish Jessica would get tired of talking about that stupid letter from Lois Lattimer."

Mr. Clark had written to Lois Lattimer about Jessica's SAVE THE TREES campaign, and two days before, a letter had arrived congratulating Jessica on raising the environmental consciousness of Sweet Valley Middle School.

True to form, Jessica had been talking about it nonstop. Elizabeth shook her head and began to shovel dirt around the base of the newly planted tree.

"Great pass!" they heard Denny shout to Aaron as Denny ran down the sideline of the new soccer field.

Janet stepped across the bulldozed field that had once been the woods. Mary, Tamara, and several of the other Unicorns were walking with her.

Janet squinted toward the soccer field, where the boys were practicing for their upcoming game.

"Denny is really playing well," Amy said.

"They're all playing really well," Lila said.

"They ought to be," Elizabeth said with a laugh. "They've been practicing night and day."

"I know," Janet said in a tight voice. "Denny is

so into soccer, he hasn't called me once this week."

"None of the guys seem to be interested in us anymore," Tamara complained. "It sort of makes me sorry they ever got to Division A."

"I know what you mean," Ellen Riteman said dejectedly.

"I wish there were something going on to get their minds off of soccer," Kimberly Haver said.

"The annual charity carnival is coming up in three weeks," Mary said. "Everybody always gets really psyched about that."

"Hey, that's right!" Janet said, brightening. "And it's up to the Unicorns to come up with the coolest booth, just like we do every year."

"Remember our sundae-making booth last year?" Grace Oliver asked.

"That was hilarious!" Betsy Gordon said.

"So what are we going to do this year?" Jessica asked excitedly.

What will the Unicorns plan for the annual Middle School charity carnival? Find out in Sweet Valley Twins No. 72, THE LOVE POTION.

Created by FRANCINE PASCAL

Jessica and Elizabeth Wakefield have had lots of adventures in *Sweet Valley High* and *Sweet Valley Twins* . . .

Now read about the twins at age seven! All the fun that comes with being seven is part of *Sweet Valley Kids*. Read them all!

Created by FRANCINE PASCAL

Don't miss the extra-long special editions of this top-selling teenage series starring identical twins Jessica and Elizabeth Wakefield and all their friends.

SUPER EDITIONS

> The Class Trip
> The Unicorns Go Hawaiian

SUPER CHILLERS

> The Ghost In the Graveyard
> The Carnival Ghost
> Ghost In The Bell Tower